INVISIBLE
INC

To Ruben - go, Mango!
Steve Cole

For Tony
Jim Field

OTHER STORIES BY STEVE COLE:

STOP THOSE MONSTERS • *MAGIC INK* • *ALIENS STINK*
ASTROSAURS • *COWS IN ACTION* • *SLIME SQUAD*
TRIPWIRE • *YOUNG BOND*

A MAGIC INK PRODUCTION • FIRST PUBLISHED IN GREAT BRITAIN IN 2016 BY
SIMON AND SCHUSTER UK LTD • A CBS COMPANY • • 10 9 8 7 6 5 4 3 2 1
SIMON & SCHUSTER UK LTD • 1ST FLOOR, 222 GRAY'S INN ROAD, LONDON
WC1X 8HB • WWW.SIMONANDSCHUSTER.CO.UK • SIMON & SCHUSTER AUSTRALIA, SYDNEY
SIMON & SCHUSTER INDIA, NEW DELHI
WWW.MAGICINKPRODUCTIONS.COM
A CIP CATALOGUE RECORD FOR THIS BOOK IS AVAILABLE FROM THE BRITISH LIBRARY.
PB ISBN: 978-0-85707-876-6 • EBOOK ISBN: 978-0-85707-877-3

PRINTED AND BOUND BY CPI GROUP (UK) LTD, CROYDON, CR0 4YY

SIMON & SCHUSTER

Have you noticed

...how no one ever goes to the toilet in action stories?

Secret agents never arrive at a glamorous hotel busting for a wee.

Batman's never got diarrhoea when the bat signal goes up.

And in spooky tales no one ever gets so scared that they stop the action for a loo break. You'd think the characters would be wetting themselves throughout – but no!

Why is that?

No idea.

Or to put it in a picture:

That's me. Noah Deer. Sounds like 'No Idea' – get it? My parents' attempt at a brilliant joke. Perfect for so many occasions, such as:

Ahh, how Mum and Dad must have laughed about my name, before they grew to hate each other and break up when I was small!

Anyway, I always thought that if I ever wrote an action story, I would keep it real and mention how many times the hero went to the toilet when it wasn't necessary to the plot (or to set up a comedy death).

Then one day my life became an action story.

And it's been tough. In all kinds of ways. Although, weirdly, remembering when I went to the toilet wasn't one of them – as you'll find out.

Can't wait, eh?

Come on, turn the page already!

INVISIBLE INC.

– and so it begins...

CHAPTER ONE

Haunted by a Tin of Beans

I was just washing my hands after my morning wake-up wee (see? Nothing glossed over) when I heard something downstairs.

It sounded like someone was throwing stuff around the living room.

"Mum?" I called. She was the only one in – it was just me and her living in that creepy old house – but I didn't expect her to answer. Mum kind of lives in her lab in the basement. She doesn't hear a thing down there with her music on.

Mum is an inventor and, when she gets on the scent of a discovery, that's it. She seems to forget I'm even here – just leaves a supply of baked beans on the kitchen worktop so I can feed myself while she's working.

Anyway, I could still hear weird stuff downstairs. Glass breaking. Things banging against the wall.

We've got burglars! I thought. *Or . . . more likely . . .*

Ghosts!

I was glad that I'd just emptied my bladder.

It may sound crazy, but, since we'd moved into our latest house at the start of the summer holidays, I had the weirdest feeling that I was being watched. The fact that our new house was an old, dark, creepy Victorian lodge – in the overgrown grounds of an old, even darker and creepier abandoned stately home – made things worse, as you can imagine. I was just glad the place had a toilet upstairs and downstairs, so a 'wee of fear' was always an option.

But yes. Invisible things, watching me. That was the feeling I got from this place.

I crept slowly down the stairs, hoping I'd meet Mum on her way up from her lab to investigate who – or what –

was wrecking the living room. But, as I peeped through the open doorway, I realised that would be difficult.

Because Mum was wrecking the living room.

"Yeahhhhh!" Dressed in her usual skinny blue jeans and white leather lab coat, she was dancing about with a bulging bin bag over her shoulder. There was rubbish all over the floor, and she wasn't stopping there: "Taste my slop, sofa cushions!" She reached into the bag, pulled out a half-empty Pot Noodle and chucked it onto the sofa. "Oh, okay, armchair, you wanna piece of this action?"

I wish I could say I was shocked and dismayed by my mother's behaviour but, to be honest, she's often like this. She calls it 'not pandering to society's expectations of a woman in her forties'. I call it 'totally embarrassing'.

I watched her empty a tin of paint over the log basket. "Ha, now how about you, TV?"

"STEP AWAY FROM THE TELEVISION!" I threw myself in front of it. With Mum working late every night, the telly was all I had for company; I wasn't about to let it get coated in something gunky. "Mum, please, calm down. I know you've been working hard—"

"Hard?" she cried. "You have no idea!"

"No, YOU have Noah Deer," I corrected her (punning cunningly). "I'm your son, remember? You have a son, Mum, and you're freaking him out."

"Don't be afraid, darling. I have to make the mess so that I can get rid of it!" She grinned at me, brown eyes wide and staring. "And I will, just you wait. **I'm going to get rid of ALL the rubbish!"**

Sometimes I have to remind myself who's the parent and who's the child. "Mum," I said patiently, "throwing it round the house is not getting rid of it. Now why don't I get you some water?"

"Water's no good!" Mum cried. "Get me something that will stain!"

"What?"

"Bring some red wine!"

"Mum, maybe you've had too much red wine already?"

"I haven't touched a drop!" Mum was skipping round the room, dancing with her smelly bin bag. "But if this thing works, I'm going to crack open the champagne!"

Man, she'd really flipped this time. Since the TV no longer seemed in imminent danger, I figured it was best to fetch that glass of water after all and hope it might calm Mum down a little.

So I headed through the draughty hall towards the kitchen. How I hated that old, cold kitchen with its freezing slate floor and big, black-leaded oven thing and the wooden worktops crowded with bean tins and . . .

I froze.

Stared.

Felt hairs stand up on the back of my neck and chills prickle my spine.

On the worktop, before my startled eyes, a tin of beans was shaking in a sinister fashion.

Suddenly it floated into the air and bobbed towards me . . .

CHAPTER TWO

This House is Haunted

(not necessarily by beans, but I'm not ruling them out)

Unless you've ever gone up close and personal with a floating tin of beans, it probably doesn't sound that scary. Beans aren't famed for their spine-tingling nature.

But it wasn't the tin that was worrying me. It was the unknown **THING** waving the tin in my face.

I couldn't see anything, but I knew it had to be **A GHOST!**

I just knew it! I thought (in between thinking *ARRRRRRRRGH* and *NOOOOOOOOOOOOOOOOO* and *OMG, OMG, OMG-eeeeeeeeeee!*). *I KNEW a ghost would show up in this creepy house sooner or later!*

Suddenly the tin dropped to the floor and burst open. Beans went splattering over the kitchen floor to their doom.

I stared at the mess, still frozen in shock.

That feeling I told you about – the feeling I was being watched? Well, I felt it right then. A sense that we weren't alone, Mum and me. I'd had it for ages.

It was nothing I could really pin down: a creaky floorboard at night (okay, I suppose I could pin down the floorboard, in theory) . . . ornaments vanishing from one room and turning up in another (yes, all right, I suppose I could pin down some of the ornaments as well) . . . things going missing without explanation (including the drawing pins I used to put up posters in my room; I couldn't pin pins down, could I? Clever-pants!).

Then there was that freaky feeling I told you about: the feeling that I was being watched.

Why did Mum choose such a spooky place for us to live, you might ask?

Well, after she broke up with Dad, she was going to buy a modern house with loads of cool kit for her work.

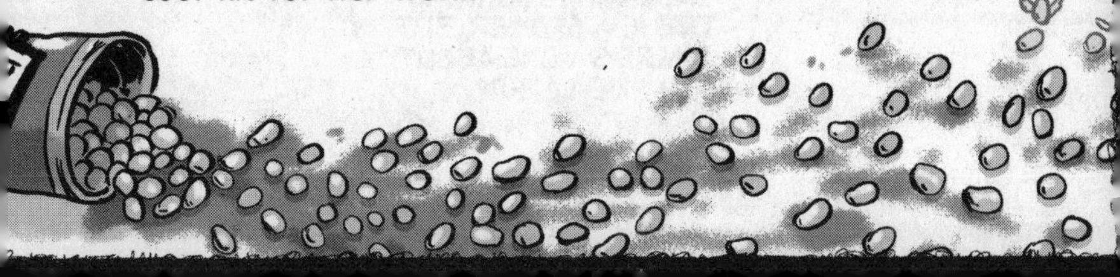

Then she found that this place was for rent, and that the stately home in the grounds was once owned by her all-time idol – a posh Victorian scientist who broke all the rules, Baroness Jemima Smyth. We have her picture on the wall.

Anyway, let's get back to things in the kitchen. I was still staring at the bean can of big-time spookiness when I caught a movement behind me.

ARRRRRRRRRGH!!!

But it was only Mum.

"Noah!" she cried. "Ooooh. You've made a mess!"

Next thing I knew, she was pointing a gun at me!

It wasn't your typical gun – the sort that a gangster or space alien might use. This thing looked part vacuum cleaner, part supermarket checkout scanner and part laser gun with a small hourglass wired into the middle.

"Mum, don't shoot!" I squeaked. "I know you're kind of stressed and I'm sorry there's a mess, but—"

"You did great, Noah!" Mum jumped over the beans spill and grabbed one of the tins. "Now, prepare to be shocked."

"I already am shocked!" I told her. "I didn't do this. The beans sort of lifted into the air and—"

"Anti-gravity beans, huh? Wow! Great idea, Noah. I'll make a note." She nodded distractedly, aiming her weird gadget at the mess on the floor. "Now! First, I scan your low-sugar baked haricot beans in tomato sauce and their tinplate container . . ."

"Mum, listen—!"

"It's all right, Noah, I'm not cross with you." Mum's gadget beeped and flashed red. "You're giving me another chance to demonstrate the scientific mega-breakthrough that is the Scan-and-Zapper!"

"What?"

"You're giving me another chance to demonstrate the scientific mega-breakthrough that is the Scan-and-Zapper!" She nodded solemnly. "I cherish that gift."

"Please, Mum," I said through gritted teeth, "I've just seen a tin of beans—"

ZAPPPPPP! I flinched and closed my eyes as Mum's gizmo fired a burst of bright red light.

"Tin of beans?" She grinned. "What tin of beans?"

I frowned. "Er, that tin of beans." I pointed to the mess, still on the floor. "The tin just rose up into the—"

"Ohhh, I'm such a div!" Mum groaned. "I forgot to switch on the Scan-and-Zapper's power source – to make short work of the tomato sauce, aha ha!" She pressed some buttons and held her gizmo like a guitar.

"C'mon!"

ZAPPPPPP! The bright red light fired again. This time I was prepared and kept my eyes wide open.

And . . . whoa!

I stared, so amazed that even thoughts of the sinister bean poltergeist took a back seat for now.

The dented can and its saucy splatter had disappeared!

"Where did it go?" My world was rocked. "Things can't just vanish into nothing!"

"That's exactly what I thought," said Mum. "Things can't just vanish into nothing. It makes a mockery of the laws of physics."

"So what happened to the beans, then?"

"I think they just vanished into nothing." Mum shrugged. "Unless maybe they were sent to another dimension . . ."

"You mean you don't know?"

"Not exactly! Not yet." Mum laughed and walked back to the living room. "But I know that those beans no longer exist in our world. And neither does that gunky trash I threw all over the place . . ."

Still stunned, I followed her to find the paint and gunk and Pot Noodle had all gone. The room was rubbish-free.

"How were you able to do this?" I asked.

"Being a genius helps! And knowing a genius helps, too. Or sort of knowing one."

"Mum, are you trying to be mysterious?"

"I don't know, Noah." Mum raised an eyebrow. **"AM I???"** Then she headed for the hall and the doorway to her basement lab. "I must get back to work. Can you make your own tea tonight? There are plenty more tins of beans on the kitchen worktop."

I grabbed her lab coat. "Mum, like I said before – those beans you zapped on the floor. Before they got there, they were floating in the air all by themselves!"

"Ahhhh, yes, the anti-gravity beans!" Mum kissed my head. "I love your imagination."

"I mean it! It was like a ghost was waving them in my face!"

"Right. Of course. Well, tell the ghost to push off – those beans are yours." Mum winked at me. "Oh, and Scan-and-Zapper sucks as a name, don't you think? See if you can think of a better one." She waved and crossed to the door of her lab. "Now I really must find out more about this zapping process."

"Find out?" I frowned. "You invented it, didn't you?"

"Er . . . yes. Obviously." Mum looked shiftily from side to side. "And it's a good job someone as lovely as me did invent it. In the wrong hands, the Scan-and-Zapper could be the most massively dangerous weapon in history . . ."

As she spoke, the door handle turned by itself. And then the door creaked open. I gasped, pointed and whimpered at this sudden super-spookiness – but Mum had already walked through and gone downstairs, lost in thought.

Once she'd gone, the door swung shut firmly behind her.

At least, it sounded like it did. I didn't actually see it.

I was already racing off to the toilet.

CHAPTER THREE

In which, Stuff that's a Bit Freaky Happens

After my toilet trip (another wee was performed), I shivered in my room under a duvet for quite a while. My mind was trying to come to terms with all I'd seen.

Had that tin of beans really floated by itself?

Had Mum really made it disappear with her 'Scan-and-Zapper' (better name to be confirmed)?

Had Mum's door really opened and closed by itself?

(Clue: Yes. Duh! Weren't you reading any of the last chapter?)

My mind had become a whirlwind of weird. Curse my

mum! Why did she have to be inspired by some dead Victorian scientist? Why couldn't someone like Tony Stark/ Iron Man have fired her up instead? Then maybe she'd have rented a flashy tower block in New York and invented a cool robot suit instead of building a high-tech bean-mop in a haunted house.

Straight away, of course, I felt bad for resenting Mum's work. It hadn't been easy for her, following her scientific dreams while looking after me. Since Dad had emigrated to the other side of the world, he hadn't been much help with the babysitting. I didn't want to add to her stress levels. Especially as this invention of hers a) actually worked and b) might make her **RICH!** Which meant no more baked beans and no more spooky little house. She'd realise at last how she'd neglected me, and to make her feel better I would allow her to shower me with fantastically expensive gifts for several years. What can I say? I'm big-hearted like that.

Meantime, she'd asked me to come up with a better name for her new invention, hadn't she? What should it be called? I wondered. How about . . .

The **Scan-o-Zap**™
The **Zapper-Scanno-Matic**™

The **Whoops**-**Where-Did-That-Thing-Go-Ray**™ (or **WWDTTG-Ray** for short. Or, er, long. Why does 'W' take so long to say? Curse you, letter 'W'!)

The Beam Extreme™ (simple but effective)

Beam Removing Intricate Atoms in Nanoseconds™ (or **BRIAN**™ for short)

The **WHAAAAAAAAAAAAAAAAAT? HOW-THE-WHAT-DID-THAT-DID-YOU-SEE-HUH???**™

In fact, the more I thought about Mum's amazing invention (you know, to try and take my mind off GHOSTS), the more my mind went, *WHOA there, soldier!*

Think of the possibilities! You could do amazing, incredible, impossible things with a **BRIAN**™. I mean, for starters you could:

• Scan nasty, horrible viruses and diseases and zap them out of a patient's body!

• Scan atomic bombs and zap them out of existence!

• Scan the smoke pouring out of factory chimneys and zap it to stop the pollution!

• Scan your wee and poo and then zap yourself every morning so you don't need to waste time going to the toilet any more! (Note: *This would also make action stories more believable.*)

• Scan your most unfair and rubbish teacher and zap him or her into nothingness!

Of course, I was just daydreaming about teacher-removals. I meant it as a joke. But then it hit me, what Mum had said: *In the wrong hands, the Scan-and-Zapper could be the most massively dangerous weapon in history . . .*

Never mind teacher-removal. I imagined armies fighting wars: thousands of soldiers, each armed with a **BRIAN™**, zapping each other out of existence . . . I pictured mad world-rulers vanishing the water supplies of their enemies so whole populations would die of thirst . . . or a crazy supervillain splatting the sun and the skies going dark . . . or—

Suddenly my phone buzzed and rang. I jumped about a mile, but once I'd scraped my nerves off the ceiling I was quite looking forward to a call from whoever was on the line: one of my old mates I'd left behind, maybe, or . . .

No.

There was no name or number on the screen. Only four words: **You are in danger**

"AAAAGHH!" I threw the phone across the room. Unfortunately, it bounced off the wall and hit me on the head. "OWWWW!"

The phone fell onto the floor. Then it stopped ringing.

I peered down. The words had gone.

"I . . . I must've imagined it." Cautiously, I reached down and picked up the phone again.

Another message appeared:

Do not make me wave more beans in your face in an attempt to get your attention!

"AAAAAGHHHH!" I screamed, and threw the phone at the wall again. This time I didn't stick around for the ricochet, I just ran from the room and pelted downstairs.

"Mum!" I rushed over to the basement door and tried the handle, but it was locked. "Mum, open up! Pleeeeeeeeease!"

THUMP. Something dropped at my feet.

My phone.

My phone that I had just left back in my room.

"AAAAAAAAAGHHHHH!" I yelled – my third scream in as many minutes (and my finest, too!). I stared down at the phone's cracked screen. Another text message had appeared:

Do not answer the door!

"Huh?" I said.

And then the doorbell went.

CHAPTER FOUR

A Mysterious Visitor

(and Guess What? Could it be A GHOST?)

The ring of the doorbell was a lively, electric chime, but to my ears, just then, it sounded like the clang of doom.

A ghost had taken over my phone and now it was warning me not to open the door.

Should I do what it said – as if it had my best interests at heart?

Duh, Noah! I told myself. *It's a GHOST!* It's a dread spirit from beyond the afterlife! What, you think it came here to tuck you into bed each night and read you lovely stories?

And, if this GHOST was telling me not to open the door,

it probably meant there was a ghost-hunter waiting there – or an exorcist, maybe? Someone brave and kind who could actually do something about all this blood-curdling creepiness!

I ran to the study window and saw a large rusty van in the street marked

SEERBLIGHT SOLUTIONS

FOR THE PROBLEMS YOU DON'T EVEN KNOW YOU HAVE

Weird, I thought. Then I peered to my left and saw a burly, boss-eyed man in a stained vest standing by the front door. He had a large empty sack slung over one shoulder.

The doorbell rang again. I hesitated. When it said, 'Don't answer the door', perhaps the ghost was on to something?

Or *up* to something.

"Mum!" I yelled again.

The man outside heard me shout. He looked in at me through the study window – at least I think he was looking at me. His eyes stared off in two different directions at once, and he had one of those chins that looks a bit like a bum. He grinned and waved and pulled faces like I was a little baby in a cot or something.

Verrrrrrrrry weird.

He went on waving and nodding and grinning. Awkward! Now I couldn't pretend I wasn't at home.

"Mum!" I called again. "Someone's at the door . . ."

But no, cancel that.

Someone was *opening* the door, even though it had been firmly closed. Hadn't it?

Was it the ghost again?

I hurried to the door and put my foot behind it so it couldn't open all the way. "Er . . . hello?"

"Hello, sonny," said the man in a gruff voice. "I'm Mr Butt, Head of Operations."

That took me slightly by surprise. Especially as he had the bum chin, too. "You're . . . Mr Butthead?"

"No, Mr Butt – Head of Operations at Seerblight Solutions. I've come to kidnap your mother."

My hair almost stood on end. "WHAT?"

"I said, er, I've come to gift-wrap your blubber." Mr Butt laughed nervously. "You know – whale blubber, seal blubber, dolphin blubber . . ."

"We haven't got any blubber." I gave him what I hoped was a hard stare. "And, if we did, why would we want it gift-wrapped?"

"That's why you need Seerblight Solutions!" cried Mr Butt in triumph. "For the problems you don't even know you've got. Let me see your mum so I can put her in this sack—" He broke off and cleared his throat. "I mean, explain the situation to her, ha ha."

"Mum can't be disturbed," I said, feeling really nervous now. My phone started buzzing and ringing from the floor. "I'd, er, better answer that. Bye!"

I tried to close the door, but Mr Butt kicked it open and I fell back into the hall with a cry. He stepped inside and raised the sack. "Now then. We'll go and see your mother together, shall we . . . ?"

"Nooooooooo!" Panic leapt from my brain without a parachute. "Keep away!"

But just then my ringing phone took off from the hall carpet like a rocket ship! It shot across the hall and smacked Mr Butt on the chin. **"OOOF!"** He was hit so hard he spun around on his heel through 180 degrees. Suddenly Mr Butt's butt was bearing down on me, saggy and huge, twitching as if with a life of its own. But the bottom didn't stay in my face for long: a swarm of drawing pins came flying from the living room and jabbed into his lower cheeks.

Mr Butt leapt into the air and ran out through the front door, more pins pursuing him like little brass wasps. As he left, the door swung shut by itself. ***SLAM!***

I stood there, trembling. It was about the only movement I could manage. On the one hand, I was relieved that Mr Butt had gone. On the other hand, he'd only gone because my phone and some pins had flown impossibly through the air – which made me think I ought to be running out after him.

My phone had stopped ringing; it lay silent and still, smoke rising from the case. I touched it but quickly snatched back my fingers. It felt red-hot.

What was going on around here?

"Mum!" I yelled, and ran down into her lab.

CHAPTER FIVE

"Mum! Right! Answers! Now! Let's Go!"

I'd had enough! The weird stuff around here had gotten worse since Mum started zapping things into nothingness. Coincidence? *NO*-incidence! (Ha ha, I am funny.) So, as you can see from the picture, I barged down those stairs meaning business.

Sadly, Mum's busyness meant she didn't notice, especially since she was working with her headphones on. *Grrrrrr*. This was her space – the **Mum-Cave**, she often called it – a mashed-up mixture of hyper-high-tech stuff and out-of-date oddities. Various computers sat on lab benches between bubbling beakers and test tubes, while centrifuges and electron microscopes shared shelf space with sextants and dusty old books.

"What's going on, Mum?" I gave her my most impassioned look. I'm sure she would have been struck by its intensity and longing if she'd bothered to look up from her microscope.

"Sorry, li'l dude, what was that?" Mum nudged her headphones off her ears. "Bit busy right now. Have we run out of beans?"

"Stuff the beans!"

"You want stuffed beans? Okay, next time I order online—"

"I want you to SPILL the beans."

Mum looked back into her microscope. "But I cleared up the spilled beans, love . . . remember?"

"That does it. I'm taking a hostage." I snatched up the nearest thing on her desk – a small jar, a quarter filled with white powder. "Stop work and talk to me, or I . . ." I shook the jar over my head. "I'll chuck this stuff down the toilet!"

Mum glanced up at last – and, like a cartoon, her eyes seemed to bulge out of her head. **"NOAH!"** She tore off her headphones, shaking and pale. "Noah . . . put down that Salt of Igneous!"

Something told me this wasn't the sort of salt you dipped your chips in. "Huh?"

"It's the power source of my **Scan-and-Zapper**." Mum was speaking quietly, through gritted teeth. "When excited correctly, it makes things disappear. When excited *in*correctly, it could go off like a bomb and disintegrate the entire area."

"Ah." Slowly, very slowly, I put down the jar. "In other words – *pow*-powder, huh?"

"Ooh, pow-powder!" Mum perked up suddenly. "Yeah, man, that rocks! Modern. Snappy." She mimed a guitar solo that made me cringe. **"RIGHT ON!"**

"I was also thinking you could call your **Scan-and-Zapper** the **Beam Removing Intricate Atoms in Nanoseconds**™ – or **BRIAN**™ for short."

"Oooh, that's cool, too! **BRIAN**™ makes the Scan-and-Zapper sound pretty friendly – for such a devastatingly destructive device."

I nodded. "With pow-powder powering it, no wonder my haunted phone told me I was in danger."

Mum frowned. "Your *what* now?"

Finally, I had her attention! Before she could take it away again, I held out my poor bust-up phone and quickly offloaded all the weirdness I'd gone through since my close encounter of the bean kind.

Once I'd finished, Mum just stared at me. She looked kind of guilty and a bit disappointed. "Oh, Noah. I know I've been working too much lately, and you're missing my attention, but to break your own phone to try and support such a crazy story . . ."

"I'm not making this up! It really happened."

"Be patient for just a while longer, okay?" Mum's eyes were pleading. "I need just a little more time to learn how to reverse the effects, then I'll be ready to present pow-powder to the world. Just think, your old mum will be famous and we'll be rich!"

"Does that mean we can move out of this dump?"

"This 'dump' is the reason it's happening! I'd never have stumbled on pow-powder if I hadn't had help . . . help from a long, long time ago." Mum pulled a key from her pocket, unlocked a drawer in her desk and pulled out an old, leather-bound notebook. "Help from my heroine –

Baroness Jemima Smyth!"

Wow, I thought (sarcastically, obvs). *An old book.* "Did you buy it on eBay or something?"

"I found it here in this room, under a broken floorboard." Mum pointed to a corner where a chunk of wood was missing. "It's a kind of work diary from 1869 . . ." Mum waved the book around.

By bombarding pow-powder with light and energy she could make close-by objects disappear...

Jemima continued her experiments until she died suddenly in unexplained circumstances.

"That's a bit creepy," I murmured. "Finding her secret notebook after all this time."

"It's almost as if it found me." Mum beamed. "Suddenly I had the chance to finish my heroine's work! Modern technology makes it much easier to simulate pow-powder, and by adding a scanner – **YEAHHH!** – I can make sure I don't vanish something important by mistake. Like the ceiling. Or you."

"Being vanished might not be so bad," I said, finding a smile. "I wouldn't have to eat beans any more. And if that weirdo Mr Butt comes back here . . ."

"Noah, I told you—"

"He was really here! He came in a van marked Seerblight something or other."

"What did you say? Seerblight?" Mum flicked through the pages of the old diary. "Well, isn't that curious? Look here. The last entry . . ."

She held up the book and, as I read Baroness Jemima's final words, my spine buzzed like there was a fly trapped inside it:

I know that Seerblight will visit me again . . .

Mum shrugged. "Funny coincidence, huh?"

Funny?

I didn't crack a smile all the way back upstairs to the toilet.

CHAPTER SIX

What I Saw When I Was Playing Video Games

I sat in the living room and switched on the TV for company. But really I didn't take in a word. My mind was too busy wrestling with mysteries – and coming off worst.

A hundred and fifty years or so ago, Seerblight Solutions had called on Baroness Jemima at her home. Why?

Today, they had called on me and Mum, right here at Baroness Jemima's old house. Why?

WHHHHHYYYYYYYYYYYY?

Pow-powder. That was the only link I could think of.

Did Mr Butthead-of-Operations want to steal the pow-powder?

How did he know what Mum was up to?

I groaned. Like a mosquito in an Olympic-sized swimming pool, I felt totally out of my depth.

Just who was the ghost? Mum thought I was making the whole thing up, but I knew whose name topped my list of suspects.

Had the spirit of the long-dead baroness led Mum to her notebook hidden under the floorboards, hoping she would continue work on the pow-powder? What had Seerblight done to her – and was he/she/it/they planning to do the same to Mum and me?

I was totally creeping myself out. It was time to take action. (After I'd been to the toilet for 'a long sit'.)

After I'd been to the bathroom and washed my hands, I locked every door and window in the house. Then I cracked open some (non-floating) beans and ate them cold from the can with a fork. I left a light on in every room. I stuck some dance music in the CD player and turned the TV on at high volume, too, so it sounded like the house was full of people and we were all having an amazing party.

My plan was to leave everything on all night, to deter any unwelcome callers. Who in their right mind would try to break into a house full of people, eh? Unless they wanted to dance and party, of course.

After a bit, I got fed up with all the noise so I went to my room. My phone wasn't working, but I still had the iPad. So I killed time on that (and hoped dead time wouldn't come back to haunt me).

I did a bit of spook-browsing online.

First, I looked up Seerblight Solutions. But that brought up nothing.

Next, I typed in:

Baroness Jemima Smyth

I paused, then got more specific:

Baroness Jemima Smyth Dead Ghost

I hit '**GO**'.

And the iPad went. It flipped apps: the search engine got lost and Maps launched instead.

"Huh?" I stared at the screen, hairs prickling on the back of my neck. Typed into the search bar were the words:

Baroness Jemima Smyth Dead Ghost

A red pin with **BJSDG** written in it was sticking out

from the map on the screen.

A map that showed our house and the area around it.

"Gulp!"

Something had been typed in the Directions box:

Do not leave your house

Suddenly it felt as though my spine was the map, with tingles marking the way from one end to the other. *Show the message to Mum*, I thought – but then the iPad went dead, even though it had loads of charge. I stared at it, completely spooked. Then I hid it behind some books on the shelf.

"I'm *not* leaving the house, Baroness Smyth!" I called out. "But I really hope you do!"

No one and nothing replied.

I sighed. I needed distraction. Screen games. Lots of them.

I came back down into the noisy living room and decided to work out my frustrations with *Aliens on the Brink* – a first-person shooter game. A couple of years back, Mum made me a game controller that looks like a gun, so I can channel my negativity by zapping ugly green aliens over and over.

And so, innocently occupied in blowing the hell out of creatures from another world, I was able to forget my troubles for a time. I even turned off the stereo so I could better hear the ZAPPP! ZAPPPP! AROOOOOOOOOO! WOW-WOW-WEEEEEEEEEP! SPLAMMO! as I waved my gun at the TV, shooting those aliens . . .

Suddenly, as if pushed by invisible hands, the TV jumped off the stand. It hit the floor, and the screen exploded into glass and plasma, while I screamed and leapt backwards onto the sofa.

I found myself staring at a massive sword – floating by itself in the middle of the room!

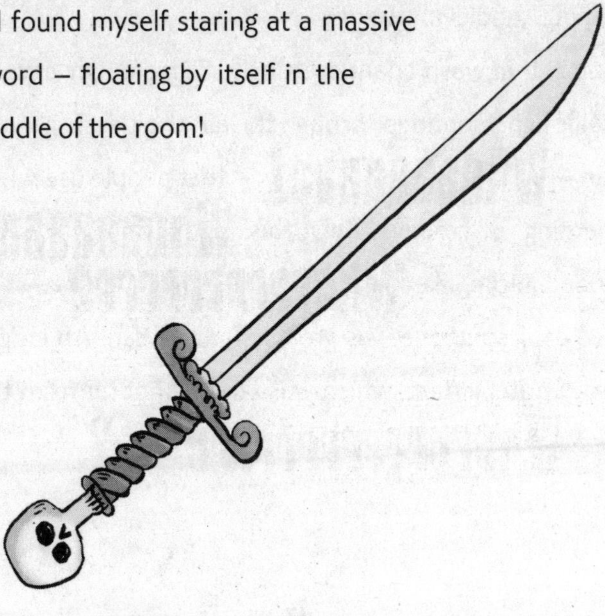

CHAPTER SEVEN

Coulda, Shoulda – Didn't

A tin of beans floating in the air is one thing. But a huge, gleaming, medieval sword?

And, if that wasn't pant-wettingly scary enough, a weird metallic echo sounded through the air: the classic ghostly groan – **Whoaaaaaaa!** – that people use when something is creepy. Only this **Whoaaaaaaa** sounded more like **Wherrrrrrrrrre—?** It was as if someone was groaning into a can. An empty can of Sprite, in fact, which was floating not far from the sword. **Wherrrrrrrrrrrre—?**

I watched in horror as the blade rose up through the air, and then screamed as it knocked the gun-controller from my hand. **Wherrrrrrrrre—?**

Then the noise cut off and both the Sprite can and the sword fell onto the coffee table, shattering the glass.

The crash was like a starting pistol (a strange starting pistol that made the sound of breaking glass instead of a gunshot, but there you go). I bolted from the room to fetch Mum.

But there was more weirdness waiting in the hallway. A clattering, clumping racket like someone was stomping in iron shoes all over the kitchen tiles.

No, not someone. An animal. It sounded like a horse.

It was the ghostly clatter of a ghostly horse's ghostly hooves!

And it was also the straw that broke the camel's back.

The combination of ghostly bean tins, phantom phones, spooky swords and now a zombie death-horse was finally enough to tip me over the edge from 'fairly terrified' into full-on 'EEEEEEEEEEEEEEEK-wibble-wobble-I-am-a-teapot' mode.

In a blind panic, I ran to the front door.

I threw open the front door.

I sprinted from the house, into the night, down the winding drive.

I charged out into the road and kept running.

Until suddenly I skidded to a stop.

Because a Seerblight Solutions van was parked in front of me.

An *empty* Seerblight Solutions van.

Which meant that if Mr Butt had been inside the van, he

was now out of it.

Three guesses where he must be headed. (*Guess 1*: Luxembourg? No. *Guess 2*: A transport café on the M4? No. *Guess 3*: My house? Yes! Oh, yes!)

Oh, no.

I hadn't passed him on my way here, so he must've been hiding. Waiting for his chance to get inside . . .

And what doofus had just run out and left the front door wide open, leaving Mum alone in the basement?

(*Guess 1*: You got it. Me!)

"Mum!" I ran back the other way, as fast as I could go. What should I do? Phone the police? Yes – however crazy things sounded, they would have to help, right? That's what I told myself. But when I got back, breathless, the front door was closed – and locked.

I felt sick. This isn't happening! None of this can be happening! I banged on the door, but of course no one opened it. I thought I could hear someone shouting. "Mum?" I whumped the wood so hard I thought my fists might fall off. "Are you—?"

The latch rattled and the door suddenly swung open. Maybe the ghosts were back on my side? I didn't much care; I just wanted to find my mum. The door to the basement was standing wide open. The strong light from the lab below sent struggling shadows dancing on the hall wall.

Mum was in trouble.

There was a loud crash and a man's shout. It sounded like Mr Butt. Maybe he was the one in trouble? Mum used to do self-defence classes – until she got thrown out for excessive violence . . .

I knew I had to do something. I should've gone straight

to the cordless phone in the living room. I should've called for help and then gone down to check on Mum.

Coulda, shoulda— Didn't.

"MUMMMMM!!!" I ran down the stairs two at a time and charged into the lab. What an action hero!

An action hero stopped in his tracks by a dazzling red light that was being shone in his eyes.

"Noah, get out!" I heard Mum bellow. "This madman's scanned you with the **BRIAN™!**"

Which isn't something you hear every day. Blinded by the scan-light, I froze in panic. Should I dive for cover, or turn and try to get out before 'this madman' pulled the trigger?

Too late. My ears rang with the same heavy-duty ***ZAP*** I'd heard back in the kitchen. The **BRIAN™** had been fired again!

This time, I was the target.

I fell over, but it was like I didn't hit the floor.

It was as if my senses had switched off. I couldn't see, hear, smell, taste or touch a single thing. The dark silence swamped me until—

"NOAHHHHHHHH!" I heard Mum sobbing. "You

blasted him! He's gone!"

"I'm not gone, Mum!" I blinked, wishing my sight would return along with my hearing. "I'm here!"

No one took any notice of me. "I needed to test your zapper, didn't I?" Mr Butt snarled. "Now we know we're not wasting the boss's time."

"Hey!" I tried again. "Right here! Helloooooo?"

"Well, big congrats, Professor Deer," Mr Butt went on. "All these years and no one else has come close to controlling the Salt of Igneous so well—"

"NOOOOOOOOOOOOOOOOOOOOOOOO-AHHHHHHHHHHHHHHH!" Mum wailed, ignoring him. "Where are you?"

"I'm right in front of you!" Sitting up, dazed and dizzy, my sight was slowly returning. I could see Mum, blearily, and Mr Butt beside her clutching the **BRIAN**™ in one hand.

But there was something that I couldn't see.

Something I couldn't see at all – because it was no longer there.

ME.

CHAPTER EIGHT

Like a Ghost!

(PS actually, I HATE a ghost!)

I couldn't see myself! How crazy-dumb was that? I closed my eyes for longer, then opened them again. I still hadn't come back. I could feel my arms, my legs, my face. I could feel my stomach churning. But my vision was blurred. I couldn't see myself at all.

And Mum . . . ?

Mr Butt was steering her away up the steps, along with the **BRIAN™** and the jar of pow-powder. "Mum!" I shouted. "I'm invisible!"

"Alas! That is not all you are," came a voice from behind me.

I turned dizzily. A woman dressed in white was kneeling on the floor. "W-W-W-Where'd you come from? Can you help me?"

"I've been trying to help you, Noah," she said, her voice deep and rich as a Christmas pudding. "As for your mother, I'm afraid there's nothing you can do just now."

"Thanks, anyway!" I had no time to listen to this. I tried to run up the steps – but instead I just went THROUGH them. My mind told me I was knee-deep in stonework, but I couldn't see myself, couldn't feel the steps at all. I just felt dizzy, in shock.

Of course, the steps were there. It was ME who wasn't.

"Your vision will be fuzzy for a time," said the mysterious woman, "but fret not! You'll soon see things as they truly are. Yourself included."

Even as she spoke, a mist seemed to form around me. I looked down and saw my jeans, suddenly pale and ghostly white. I couldn't see my feet in their trainers because I seemed to be standing inside the bottom step. My T-shirt appeared and I saw my arms, sprouting from the sleeves. I held one hand to my chest.

There was no ba-dump of a heartbeat.

There was nothing.

NOTHING.

NOTHING!!!
I'M A GHOOOOOOOOOOS SSSSSSSSSSST!

"No, no, no, no!" The woman was standing now. She had a round face and neat features, and like me she was slightly see-through, glowing like starlight. "You are not a ghost, Noah. Once you have adjusted to the shock of transmogrification—"

"Transmogri-what?" My brain and tongue were struggling in a freaked-out tangle. "Wait. I recognise your face." I gasped with fear. "You're B-B-B-Baroness Jemima Smyth."

"Indeed I am, Noah. In the flesh!" She frowned. "Um, sort of."

I felt scared stiff – or as stiff as you can be when you have zero substance. The baroness looked just like her portrait on the wall. She was wearing an old-fashioned checked cloak and a man's shirt and dark trousers. Her legs ended in a pair of ghostly leather boots.

"You've been haunting me! YOU'RE A GHOST!"

"I'm not, you know." With an awkward tinkle of a laugh, the ghostly woman did a small curtsey. "And I'd rather you addressed me as Lady Smyth."

"My mother told me never to talk to dead people!" Panic was returning. "Help! I'm dead! My mum's been kidnapped and I'm too dead to do anything about it!"

"Really, Noah! Such a preoccupation with death! It's not healthy."

"Healthy? I'm DEAD! Totally dead!" I was desperate to get upstairs, but nothing was happening – it was like I was trying to race up a down escalator. "And don't pretend you're not dead, too! You ARE dead. Dead as a dead maggot!"

"Well, really!" huffed Lady Smyth. "Look, if you want to move in this condition, you have to will it. Your brain will adjust in a short time and anchor your form to the floor as usual because that's what it's used to seeing. In the meantime, really focus on where you want to go. Picture yourself standing on those steps and . . ."

I tried, but it wasn't easy. I wobbled like crazy. Some of my steps fell through the stairs, others just above them. And when I reached the top I stumbled – and plunged straight through the closed door.

"I walked through solid wood," I groaned. "That's proof! I really am deaaaaaaaaaad!"

"Nonsense!" I saw the ghost of Lady Smyth gliding up the stairs towards me.

"*Nooooooooo!* Keep away!" For a moment, I thought she was obeying me, rising into the air. Then I realised that I was sinking through the floorboards, like I'd got into some ghostly lift back down to the lab. "Ugh!" It gave me such a shock I rose back up again. Desperately, I willed my feet to stick to the ground, waddled into the kitchen – and stared in amazement.

I could see them now: the beans (and their can) that Mum had zapped with the **BRIAN**™. Only now they were pale and see-through beans (and their can).

GHOSTLY beans (and their can).

What did it all mean? My brain felt overloaded. I couldn't think straight. I floated weightlessly through the kitchen wall and outside, onto the dark driveway, just as I had about five minutes ago. Only this time everything was different. I couldn't feel my heart pounding. There was no scrunch of footsteps on the gravel path, and my trainers left no mark. I couldn't feel the cold of the night air, couldn't smell the conifers' Christmas smell as I turned onto the main road. There was no saliva in my mouth, nothing to swallow. And I wasn't out of breath. I wasn't sure if I was even breathing at all . . .

Then I heard an engine start, up ahead: the Seerblight van pulling away from the kerb and rumbling off down the road.

"Mum!" I realised with a jolt that even if I caught up with her – what could I do? She couldn't see me. Or hear me. I would go right through her – or anything else for that matter.

"Don't be afeared." Lady Smyth had caught up with me. "Seerblight won't hurt your mother: he needs her genius. She's no use to him dead."

"Dead like me, you mean!"

"YOU'RE NOT A GHOST, Noah. Try touching your arm."

I did. My arm felt squashy under my fingers. I could hardly feel the pressure, but at least it was something.

"Now," said Lady Smyth, "the truth, in fact, is quite simple: the Salt of Igneous – pow-powder I believe you call it? – has transformed you into a state of being not typical of life on this planet."

"But very typical of *death* on this planet." I looked at her suspiciously. "You look just like a ghost. All old-fashioned and stuff."

"Old-fashioned? I'll have you know this ensemble was thrillingly modern for a girl in 1869!" Lady Smyth sighed; she really did sound uber-posh. "Alas, when I was zapped by pow-powder, my clothes became as insubstantial as I. One cannot change one's attire in this condition. In fact, one is properly lumbered with it."

"So it was pow-powder that made you disappear?" I nodded slowly. "Like the beans."

"Good lad. Now you're using your brains." She looked at me solemnly. "We are beyond human perception now, existing on a higher etheric plane."

I wasn't using my brains *that* much. "Huh?"

"Put simply, the pow-powder has turned us invisible and untouchable – at least as far as the real world is concerned." She sighed. "In this intangible state, you can no longer age or decay with the passing of time."

I chewed over this information like it was a salad – with zero enthusiasm, pulling a face. "You mean, from now on I'm never going to change? Never get any older?"

Lady Smyth gave a decisive nod. "Never."

"Then . . . I'm NOT dead!"

"Hallelujah! He grasps it at last!"

"It's more like . . . a *LIVING* death. An eternity of death!"

"Oh, dear." She groaned. "Here we go again."

She was right. There I went again.

I pegged it like the fastest zombie you ever saw, trying to keep his feet on the ground, racing off into the woods!

CHAPTER NINE

If You Go Down to the Woods Today, DON'T.

(Just don't.)

I ran and ran, through the trees – literally, whoosh!, right through the trees, like they were holograms! My brain had the brakes on while my feet were speeding up. I just couldn't get my head round everything. Kidnap! Zap! Invisible! Ghost! Not-a-Ghost! Victorian pow-powder powwow! Other stuff!

I raised my head to the night sky and yelled words I knew no one normal would be able to hear: "This . . . is . . . a . . . nightmare!"

Things were moving so fast. Even the heavy broadsword

floating in front of me was moving fast.

WAIT. What—?!

I stopped running. Stopped dead, in fact. Even though, apparently, I wasn't dead. I stopped *un*dead – sort of. Oh, **YOU KNOW WHAT I MEAN.**

"'This is a nightmare,' the boy says. Ha!" A big French-sounding voice boomed over a clopping clatter of hoofbeats. "When really it's a KNIGHT on a MARE – eh, Maloney? Not that you are a girl, of course. Ha ha ha!"

Who the heck is Maloney, you may ask? Well, I didn't at the time. All I could produce was a frightened ***"EEEEP!"*** as the pointy end of the sword sped towards me. It looked just like the one I'd seen in my living room, only this time I could see what was holding it: a pale, ghostly giant on the back of a ghostly horse, galloping through the woods towards me.

I should have wet my pants – you totally couldn't blame me. And yet I found that I couldn't even if I'd wanted to (which I didn't. Obviously). In fact, I didn't need the tiniest wee – another side effect of being powed by pow-powder! The realisation distracted me for at least 0.23 of a second as the giant raised his sword higher into the air . . .

And then dropped it to the ground.

"GAHH!" the man yelled. "A pox on these insubstantial fingers!" He pulled on the reins and his horse reared up heroically, perhaps six metres from where I stood. The big, fine-looking animal (aside from being a bit (a lot) on the see-through side) had apparently stood in some tin cans recently; its fetlocks were ghostly, but the cans on its hooves were real, like the sword. "That was a most excellent wheelie, Maloney! You're getting good."

So the horse was Maloney. But who was the man? He looked like a mountain on legs, with a beard as big as a hillside. He was dressed in a stained linen undershirt-and-pants combo and thick woollen stockings, which was nearly as upsetting as the sword.

Things got weirder. The giant swung himself down from his horse. "Lift a leg, Maloney!" The horse obliged and the man wearing underclothes carefully pulled a crumpled Coke can off the hoof. "We shall get this gun-hungering block-twizzle yet, eh, boy?"

What?! I was still holding myself motionless. Who was this guy? What was he—?

"Wherrrrrrrrrrrrre is the boy's mother, varlet?" The big man held the Coke

can to his mouth, wailing in a ghostly fashion. "Whaaaaaaat hast thou done with herrrrrrrrrrr?"

"**Whaaaaaaaaat** are you on about?" I found my voice in anger and frustration. "It's **MY** mother and I don't know where she is. Don't come shouting at me in your pants!"

The ghostly giant was so shocked he dropped his can.

"*Zut alors!* You can see me?"

"Yes, he can, Sir Guy." Lady Smyth had arrived behind me, not out of breath in the slightest. "And, if you had scared away the intruders instead of threatening the boy I asked you to protect, this woeful affair might have been avoided!"

"That was him in the lounge, then? And he was meant to protect me?" I spluttered. "He tipped over my TV while I was playing a game and nearly chopped my hand off!"

"You execute ugly green men trapped in a flat window and call it a game?" Sir Guy's beard bristled as he turned back to Lady Smyth. "You hear? The lad stands condemned by his own words. He deserved all he got! Or would've gotten if I hadn't dropped my sword!"

I looked at Lady Smyth; her neat features were pinched with sympathy. "I'm so sorry about him," she said to me.

"Is he really a knight?" I asked.

"Of course I am!" cried the knight in his fruity French voice. "I am Sir Guy deYupp!" (He said 'Guy' as 'Geeee' (with a hard G).)

"Sir Guy deYupp?" I echoed.

"The same! I am the finest swordsman in the whole of

France . . . Although, it is possible that better fighters have been born in the last 500 years, I don't know. I cannot really compete these days, in my condition. Eh, *alors.*" He puffed out a breath, looking sad – then threw off his mood and started beaming again. "Anyway! This is my pony, Maloney."

Maloney whinnied and reared up again heroically in his fizzy-drink-can slippers.

I stared. "How come he can wear those things?"

"For the same reason that I can hold a sword!" Sir Guy fumbled for his weapon on the ground, but his fingers went through it. "For a time at least."

Lady Smyth smiled. "And for the same reason I can manipulate your free-roaming telephonic communication device, and hurl pins at the fundament of that beastly rogue."

"Huh?" I said.

"I took control of your mobile and stuck pins in that man's bum. Better?" Lady Smyth tutted. "You see, the only substance with which we can interact is metal – and even then not for too long at a time. Something in the atomic make-up of metallic elements forms a bridge between our insubstantial state and the physical world..."

"But you made words appear on the phone's screen."

"By manipulating the solder and silicone in its workings. I'm terribly clever, you know." She looked quite pleased with herself. "Of course, it helps having nothing to do but practise for decades at a time. Just because I'm a formless Victorian phantom doesn't mean I can't keep up to date with the latest technology."

"Nor I!" swore Sir Guy. "For instance, the biro, eh? I bet the scribes in their monasteries didn't see THAT coming. And what about the hot-air balloon? *Fantastique!* The patterns! The hot air!" He caught our looks. "Oh. Only me, then? Not fans of the big flying balloon-with-a-basket thing?"

Maloney gave a disparaging neigh.

"In any case, metal is our lifeline," Lady Smyth went on. "Though the interactions are exhausting. I was so worn out with trying to warn you, I had to send Sir Guy along to try to protect you."

"And didn't THAT work out ever so well." I stooped and tried to pick up the fallen Coke can. My fingertips tingled and the can twitched and shifted, same as when you put two magnets pole to pole. But I couldn't pick it up. "Wow. Get me."

"For a first go, it was outstanding," Lady Smyth assured me. "To interact with the old world takes time and practice."

"And HEROISM!" boomed Sir Guy.

"Well, not really." Lady Smyth frowned. "More concentration and—"

"And COURAGE!"

"Well, a certain natural aptitude is important—"

"And LINEN UNDERPANTS."

"What? Now you're just listing your favourite things."

"True! It is an old song of war I used to sing on the battlefields of my youth!"

"Oh." Lady Smyth looked worried. "Well, that's nice, but I think we should—"

"I shall sing to you now!" boomed Sir Guy.

"No, no," she said, "you really don't have to—"

But it was too late. The silence of the wood was slaughtered and the trees trembled before a sonic onslaught unlike any I had ever heard.

"OHHHHHHHHHHHHHHHHHHHHHHHHHHHHH!" Sir Guy began,

then burst into tuneless yelling:

"I asked my mama what will I be
When I am five times taller than your knee.
BE A HERO! said she.
SMITE YOUR ENEMY!
WITH A SWORD AND A MACE,
YOU CAN SMASH HIM
IN THE FACE!
OHHHHHHHHHHHHH
-oooooo-HHHHHH!
I asked my papa what will I be
When I am approximately the size
of one-sixth of that tree.
BE COURAGEOUS! said he.
BE AS BRAVE AS CAN BE!
WITH AN AXE AND A CLUB,
YOU CAN MAKE THE
BADDIE BLUB!
OOOOOOOOOOOOOOOOOOO
OOOOOOOOOOOOOH—"

"Thank you, Sir Guy," said Lady Smyth. "I think you can stop now, before you get to the linen underpants."

"Oh . . . 'tis the best verse!" Sir Guy frowned. "But you are right. It is unseemly to sing songs of courage and bravery and underpants when the boy has had such a shock." He paused. "Though at least he can't soil his own undergarments any longer!"

"Thanks." I glared at him. "I was just trying to find the positives, too."

"I shall sing to thee another time," Sir Guy threatened. "For such great attributes will be needed in our battle against the accursed cur who has brought this fate upon us."

"Seerblight." Lady Smyth's lip curled. "Yes, we'll get him, some day."

I stared at her. "You've, er, had 150 years or so now."

"Yes, well." She looked a bit shifty. "When your mother continued my research into pow-powder, I rather hoped she would discover how to reverse its effects, to make us solid and strong again."

"But wouldn't you just . . . well, shrivel up and crumble to dust or something?" I asked. "You're, er, kind of horribly old by now, you know."

"Thank you," Lady Smyth said icily. "But I told you –

insubstantial and invisible as we are, we do not wear or wither. Time and its various erosions pass us by."

"'Tis a pity, though, in a way." Sir Guy seemed to be staring past the trees, into the distance. "Imagine how fine and heroic my beard would look if it had gone on growing these past 500 years!"

I did imagine it.

And then I tried not to.

"Why has Mum been kidnapped?" I asked anxiously. "Because she can make good pow-powder? Because of the **BRIAN**™?"

Lady Smyth considered. "Very likely."

"But we're gonna get her back, yeah?" I felt kind of woozy. "Can we get going now? Find her?"

"Noah, your body is still in a state of shock." Lady Smyth gave a sympathetic smile. "We must rest before we do anything else."

"Rest? But we're made of nothing." I swayed dizzily. "There isn't anything to rest . . ."

At which point my nothingness flopped to the forest floor in serious need of rest and everything went black.

Chapter Ten

Doctor, Doctor, I'm Afraid of Back-Story! *When Did You Find This Out?* ARRRRRRGH!

Excuse me interrupting this narrative – it is I, Lady Jemima Smyth. I thought I had best take over the telling of this tale, since Noah had passed out and I know he doesn't like to skip anything. Fortunately we shall at least be spared his toilet adventures now, since he is unable to 'go' in his invisible state.

Sir Guy lifted Noah up onto Maloney – for only Invisibles can touch other Invisibles – and together, we transported him back through the woods (literally, straight through them).

Turning back to the last chapter to compare my writing style with Noah's, you might be wondering: why did his body fall to the ground if it weighed nothing? Why did it not fall through the ground and drift down to the very epicentre of the planet's core and out the other side?

The answer, I believe, is that the human mind is a thing of habit. Our minds know that if we fall over, we hit the ground. If we walk, we walk on the ground. If we go upstairs, we take it a step at a time. Our bodies may have lost all weight and substance, but our minds can't be bothered to break the habit of what we did when gravity held sway o'er our forms.

Well, anyway, we took Noah to the wonderful old stately home that was once (and still is, in fact) my dwelling-place.

Does dwelling-place have a hyphen in it or not? Hmm.

Anyway! We took the boy to the living room – or what is left of it. Although it was the middle of the night, Noah soon woke up and was able to continue the story himself . . .

*

I woke up in the dark ruin of a once grand room. The only light was the moon-glow through the broken windows; it revealed a sad landscape of splintered furniture, sagging drapes and crumbling walls.

Had I been dreaming? No. I was still pale all over, softly glowing, not completely there. All that terrible, impossible stuff had really happened after all, and now here I was – in the sort of place Dracula might think twice about visiting.

The wind blew its lonely howl through the crevices, rustling the scraps of wallpaper, but I couldn't feel it.

The floor beneath me was covered in grit from the crumbling ceiling, but I couldn't feel that either.

I could feel NOOOOTTTHHHHHHHIIIIIIIIIIING!

Lady Smyth and Sir Guy were lying on the ground, silent as shadows. Maloney was silently pacing in a corner of the room, his ghostly tail swishing from side to side. (I guess ordinary horse-in-house rules don't apply to invisible types like Maloney – you don't have to follow his back end around with a bucket.)

I touched my arms and legs and stomach, felt the pressure against my fingers. Then I touched the floor and my fingers slipped through. It was as if I was still solid, but the world had turned into pictures and thin air. When Maloney saw me sitting up, he wandered over, nudged me with his nose and gave me a little neigh. It sounds soppy, but just that brief contact was a comfort to me.

So! This part of the story is fun, isn't it? The shocked aftermath of a life-changing disaster – always a laugh to read! I could go on for pages now about how scared I was, how weird it felt not to breathe or swallow or feel hungry or wake up and find I didn't need the toilet, or how much I missed my mum and where was she now and was she okay . . . I COULD do that.

But I won't.

It's like in *Star Wars*, when Luke Skywalker gets home to find his aunt and uncle have been murdered and his house burned down. He looks a bit glum and stares into the distance, and some sad music plays, then WHOOSH!

He's off on his adventure and never mentions his poor old relatives again. Well, my own adventure was lying ahead (and hey, not wanting to rub it in, Luke, but my mum was still alive, even if she was in deep, scary trouble). I know I said I don't want to gloss over stuff (toilet trips in particular, but they were no longer happening so never mind), but I don't want to bring you down by inflicting every last sadness on you.

So. You get me when I say I was a bit like *this* about things, right?

Just imagine me doing that from time to time in the background as we carry on with the story. It shouldn't be hard.

"Aha! 'Tis time to stir!" Sir Guy opened his eyes, stretched out his arms. "Hello, lad! How do you feel?"

I did an impression of the picture you see on the previous page.

"As good as that, eh?" Lady Smyth was also awake and back on her ghostly feet. "I hope you didn't mind resting on the floor, but all the beds were stolen and sold back in 1874."

That was just too weird to respond to. I knew I had to try not to think about things too much. "Can we go find my mum, please?"

"Of course, you fret for her, *mon brave*." Sir Guy thumped a hand down on my shoulder. "But you must learn patience. You know what they say – a hurried plan is but a furtive mickle."

"*They* say that?" I looked doubtful. "Who's they?"

"Me, mainly," the knight admitted.

Thought so. I rubbed my eyes. "It's silly, but I still feel tired. How come we need sleep?"

"Sleep refreshes the mind as much as the body." Lady Smyth shrugged. "Staying awake for 150 years without a break would drive one batty."

"Or, in the case of Maloney and myself, 500 years!" Sir Guy gave a sigh. "Maloney here was Seerblight's very first victim and I his second."

I asked the obvious question: "Who even *is* Seerblight? He can't really still be alive after all that time . . . can he?"

"He is an old and powerful man," said Lady Smyth, "part scientist, part magician."

"You mean he pulls rabbits out of hats and does card tricks while wearing a lab coat?"

Lady S was not amused. "Seerblight is a master of dark magic and secret science. A gatherer of strange and uncanny secrets, once known only to the wisest of ancients—"

"And their mothers," Sir Guy added.

"No, Sir Guy, not their mothers."

"They kept secrets from their mothers?" Sir Guy looked appalled. "This is worse than I thought!"

Lady Smyth rolled her eyes. "Allow me to explain further."

"Cool," I said.

"Back in the sixteenth century, Seerblight spent decades travelling the world on a quest to find the elixir of eternal life. He was sure it must exist and was determined that he, and he alone, would possess it . . ."

He stole every hint, lead and clue connected to the secret of the elixir . . .

One ingredient was the fabled Salt of Igneous. After years of work, Seerblight succeeded in making a tiny amount!

Combining the pow-powder with other exotic ingredients, he created his Elixir Eternal!

Now Seerblight will live forever . . . but throughout the centuries, his experiments with pow-powder have never ceased!

I was puzzled. "So he's got eternal life and he wastes it mucking around with pow-powder? Why? Why not just chill out on a yacht forever or something?"

"Pow-powder is a mighty ingredient when mixed with other potions. What other powerful, as-yet-unknown uses might it have?" Lady Smyth preened a little. "What is certain is that he has sought out brilliant minds across the years to help him with his research. Brilliant minds such as mine."

"Your diary ended with Seerblight calling round to see you," I remembered. "What happened?"

"He tried to enslave her!" cried Sir Guy. "But he hasn't bothered trying to do that to anyone else for some time."

"I suppose he has found others to help him," said Lady Smyth.

"Like Mr Butt." I frowned. "How did you get away from Seerblight? How did you turn invisible?"

She cast a sidelong glance at Sir Guy. "I'd sooner not talk about that just now."

"Ha ha!" the knight cried. "I am glad that I am no head-of-the-egg! I attacked Seerblight when he made my pony, Maloney, disappear. *Quelle horreur!* I thought my stalwart steed was dead!"

"NEIGHHH!" Maloney said, as if denying it.

"Seerblight realised pow-powder's potential as a weapon," said Lady Smyth, "but it was too dangerous, too unstable. He has spent centuries seeking to control it, teasing out its secrets."

Sir Guy took up the story. "Somehow he learned that those zapped by the powder live on, as we do – out of sight, and touch, and smell and taste and hearing."

Maloney neighed.

"And out of neigh." Sir Guy gave a small bow of apology to his horse. "Seerblight found a way to see us Invisibles, using eyeglasses made from a crystal so rare, it has no name. It is known only as . . . The Rare Crystal With No Name (That May Or May Not Be Used For Eyeglasses)."

"Catchy," I said. "So, once Seerblight could see you, what did he do then?"

"He tried to catch us, or control us, or destroy us." Sir Guy nodded. "Experiments, torture and doom, that has long been the fate of those turned invisible!"

I did my face again.

"Isn't it bad enough we're stuck like this without him wanting to destroy us?" I sighed miserably. "Like we're not destroyed enough already."

"You must not think of us as destroyed, Noah," said Lady Smyth firmly. "Invisible we may be, but we still have our minds! Still we think. Still we bide our time and plot!"

Sir Guy nodded enthusiastically. "Still we sing remarkably long and detailed tales of heroic deeds!"

"*Some* of us do," Lady Smyth said pointedly. "Well, now that we know each other, Noah, please call me Jem."

"And you can call me SIR!" said Sir Guy. (I decided not to.) "Now come, Milady Jem, tell the lad the tale of how you became invisible!"

"If I do," Jem said cautiously, "do you promise not to sing the 220-verse epic song-poem you wrote to commemorate the occasion?"

"Um . . . probably."

"Very well. As a scientific genius who was also a woman, my fame spread back in the 1850s." The fire in Lady Smyth's eyes wasn't invisible, for sure. "Seerblight came to me, pretending to be a patron of science. He promised me riches if I could make a new batch of pow-powder, here in this very house – one that was more potent and less likely to explode with hideously catastrophic results."

"Can't blame him for trying," I said. "What happened?"

"It exploded with hideously catastrophic results," she said. "I was made . . . invisible. When Seerblight found my lab in pieces, he took out his scrying glass made from The Rare Crystal With No Name and saw me, even in my invisible state. He tried to *capture* me—"

"—but I rescued you!" Sir Guy punched the air. "In a very stylish and heroic fashion!"

Jem lowered her voice. "Maloney basically got a tin stuck on one hoof and accidentally kicked a table over."

I winced. "Two hundred and twenty verses about that?"

She nodded. "Pray you never have to count them."

I turned to Sir Guy. "How come you were even there?"

"Ah. This is because of Maloney's mighty nose. It can sniff out pow-powder from very far away. So, ever since 1516 when **POOF!** we were pow-powed ourselves, he and I sniff out and try to rescue those poor souls who are also invisible but lack my skills and heroism."

I noticed he'd said "*try* to rescue". That suggested a less than 100% success rate. "What did Seerblight use to attack you—?"

My sentence was obliterated by an echoing **BAMMMM**.

Jem frowned. "That was the front door."

Sir Guy was already charging out to the hall. Jem and I followed him – me through the doorway (for old time's sake) and her through the wall – in time to see SOMETHING blow inside: a weird, multicoloured whirlwind with lumps in. Wet, gooey lumps, as big as a person.

Ohhhhhhhhhhhhh, no.

"These monsters are what he used to attack us!" Sir

Guy looked grim and Maloney reared up, waving both hooves. "They are Seerblight's servants!"

The lumps grew harder, solid as iron, as the swirl of colours faded. Now three towering horrors stood in the hallway, watching us through dark, square-lensed glasses. It was probably a good job I couldn't still go to the toilet. I was so scared I couldn't move.

The creatures walked on pointy claws. They had no feathers, only rusty metal wings with spikes. Their flesh was pink and puckered like they'd been plucked, their tails were like fountains of steel wool and their heads were made extra-horrible by their big misshapen beaks.

One of those whopping beaks opened up with a high-pitched, menacing, SQUAWK.

"BUUKKKKKK!"

"Poultry-geists," breathed Jem. "Part devil-chicken, part hunting-beast."

I groaned. "But I thought Seerblight wasn't bothered about you any more?"

"Indeed, that is so," Jem agreed. "But perhaps he is bothered about YOU."

Shrieking and clucking and pecking the air, the giant, chickeny monsters thumped towards me.

My knees knocked madly. "I think you're right, Jem. They're after me!"

Suddenly one of the poultry-geists turned round, raised its steely tail feathers – and fired an egg! The egg broke at my feet and a mess like molten metal surged out. It hardened round my ankles.

"I'm stuck!" I shouted.

The next moment, another egg was fired – and this one looked to be *solid* metal. It hit me on the head.

I heard Sir Guy shout, "Sorcery! Witchcraft! Egginess!"

None of those sounded much like fun, but I didn't get to learn a lot more, first hand. My head went **PHUT** – and switched off.

Chapter Eleven

Panic (and Something Else) Amongst the Devil-Chicken-Hunting-Beasts, as told by a Totally Street Victorian Laydee

Poor, dear Noah! Struck by two evil eggs and out for the count.

Yes, I'm back to do the narrating as Noah was asleep at the time. I will try my best not to tell you what happened in an old-fashioned manner. Yes, although I hail from the Victorian era, I am rather good with your Elizabethan slang. I have skillz. Yeah! You know it. Ooooh, how liberating it is to boogaloo with language in this way!

Sorry, I must stick to the tale in hand.

Soz.

Sozzo!

ahem

The poultry-geists scratched the floor as they bobbed closer, their metal-edged wings catching the moonlight. With those square scrying glasses they wore, the evil bird-beasts could see us all as plainly as I see you now! (Yes, I'm hovering just behind you. Don't look up from the page – we're getting to a 'well cool' bit.)

All three of the beasts were heading for Noah's manacled body.

Ever heroic, and rather stupid, Sir Guy stepped forward to face them. The poultry-geists might be after Noah, but they most certainly desired to do us harm, too. Sorry, that sounds somewhat undramatic. Well, then! They wished . . . to bust a cap in our butts! And not the sort of cap you wear on your head, oh, no! For in this instance 'cap' actually relates to the ignition cap at the base of a cartridge for a gun! Imagine!

Now, where was I?

Sir Guy swung his sword at the nearest poultry-geist. But the monster brought up its wing and deflected the blow, knocked the weapon from Sir Guy's grip. Maloney – well-trained as ever – put on his tin-can horseshoes and galloped over.

SCRUNCH!!

SQUAWWWRK!!

He trampled two of the beasts to the floor, yo! However, the third flapped its wings and jumped in the air, its metallic claws crunching down on the pony's back. Maloney neighed with agony, legs buckling beneath him.

"Get off him, foul beast!" Sir Guy picked up his sword and threw it like a missile, striking the ugly beast just above the beak. With a squawk, it went tumbling backwards and the scrying glasses fell from its face.

What was I doing all this while, you may ask? Well, I was not standing idle, if that's what you were thinking! This was not the first time I had faced poultry-geists. For many years in the early twentieth century, Sir Guy, Maloney and I had been forced to run and hide from the vile creatures all around the world, each time barely giving them the slip.

But though the beasts had not bothered us for many decades, and Seerblight had forgotten all about us (so I thought), I believe in being prepared. This was my manor (quite literally!). Home turf! My streets, my rulez, you get me?

I dashed to a metal cabinet in the corner and, from within, pulled out two specially prepared glass phials in metal holders. In each was a most noxious mixture of chemicals, prepared in my old laboratory at great personal expense (I can only handle my instruments using an old chain-mail glove, and even then not for very long at a time). And, as Sir Guy battled on, I took my chance – as you may witness here in this series of fine engravings:

And lo, it came to pass that the poultry-geists became inedible roast dinners. Go me, right? Respect is due!

"What happened?" Noah said, woken by the blast.

"Do not be afeared, lad!" boomed Sir Guy. "Milady was wrong to call them poultry-geists! Why, they were only chickens escaped from a farmer's field!"

"I'm not a five-year-old," Noah complained. "Just tell me, what's a poultry-geist?"

"Well, the name is of my own invention," I said, "a play on words with 'poltergeist', which is a sort of invisible ghost, and 'poultry' meaning domestic fowl such as chickens— "

"I know what poultry is!" Noah shouted. "But what were *they?*"

"Seerblight's sinister fusion of metal, flesh and magic," I explained. "They stride the divide between the real world and ours with three desires only: to peck, claw and murder us!"

"Four desires if you count the egg-chucking,"

Noah said.

Sir Guy surveyed the fried chicken bodies. "We have stopped these three, but more will come. While the boy stays here, we are targets once again!"

"Or Noah is, at any rate," I said. "Well, it seems to me we have two choices here. Either we hand Noah over to Seerblight—"

"WHAT?" Noah gasped.

"And we cannot do that, of course," I added quickly. "So the only way to protect ourselves . . ."

"Is to take the fight to him!" boomed Sir Guy. "We ATTACK! WE WAGE WAR!"

I grimaced. "Er, actually, I was going to say, 'the only way to protect ourselves is to run away'."

"I'd love to run away," said Noah, "but I can't. Seerblight's got my mum prisoner. And Mum was working on a way to reverse what pow-powder does. If we ever want to be normal again – we've *got* to get her out!"

CHAPTER TWELVE

The Trojan Chicken

I'd like to thank Lady J for stepping up to tell that part of the tale. But now I'm back! And things were getting serious. Yes, even more serious than a fight with giant chicken-monsters.

"Right, then," I said. "We can either hide in here and wait for the next poultry-geist attack, or we can DO something." I sighed, staring round at the battered chicken-beasts. "For a start, we can drag these things outside so we don't have to look at them."

"Good idea." Jem marched over to one of the poultry-geists. "You should be able to touch their metal tails, Noah . . ."

I tried to grab hold of the buckled (or buk-bukkled) metal and this time my hand actually closed round it! It was so exciting to be able to touch something again. Unfortunately, the dead poultry-geist was so heavy I could hardly shift it.

"I shall help you, *mon brave*!" Sir Guy declared heroically.

"I wonder how these things got here," I said. "I mean, did they just walk through town?"

"No doubt Seerblight transported them by magical means," said Jem, dragging her poultry-geist along. "And, if they still lived, doubtless they would depart that way as well— **GOODNESS!**"

She jumped away as a ball of flickering green light appeared around the poultry-geist. It grew stronger, brighter.

"What's happening?" I demanded.

"I'm not sure," said Jem, "but it's happening to *your* poultry-geist, too. Get back!"

But I couldn't let go. The green light was engulfing *me*, too – and Sir Guy.

"Sorcery!" he cried, unable to release the tin tail feathers of the horrible monster. "What is happening?"

"I've seen this sickly green magic before," Jem twittered.

"I fear Seerblight is recalling his servants, to see what has befallen them!"

I stared out at her through the green fog. "And . . . we're being taken with them?" I joined Sir Guy in struggling to get free, but it seemed we were powerless. Suddenly we all shot away, whooshing up through the ruined ceiling and the gloomy upstairs rooms and out into the porridgy-grey morning. So fast! It was horrible – at least twice the speed of the fastest theme-park ride ever . . . It felt like my stomach had exploded.

"Courage, *jeune homme*!" bellowed Sir Guy, as we bounced around inside the orb of light. "You said you wanted to do something to help your *maman*! Perhaps being transported magically alongside a dead chicken-monster is good?"

"How could it EVER be good?"

"If the poultry-geist is being taken back to Seerblight's camp, and if we are hitching a ride – hurrah!" Sir Guy cheered. "We are being taken straight to where your kin is . . . in the heart of our enemy's lair!"

I was so scared, I didn't know what to think. Everything was happening so fast – literally. The town and countryside streaked below me as if they were a TV advert and we were fast-forwarding through it. Ahead of me, through the first pink-gold streaks of dawn, I could make out an ultra-modern skyscraper I'd never seen before. It was a mountain of steel and glass, with a neon sign on top flashing: **SEERBLIGHT SOLUTIONS**. It was as if the landscape was an egg and the skyscraper was the beak of a ma-hoosive creature breaking through (er, with a neon sign on top).

I stared. "I never noticed this place when Mum drove me to Asda for the annual baked bean buy-up."

"Seerblight has built many lairs in many places," said Sir Guy. "Perhaps this one is new, as he has not long since arrived."

Speaking of arrivals, ours seemed imminent. I screamed as we dipped down from the sky and accelerated further, and Sir Guy joined in with a loud squeal as we shot at speed towards the ground floor, which was covered in gleaming metal shutters.

At the last second, there was a flash of light, the shutters opened up and we were in. **WHANG!** Our steaming poultry-geist flew down a kind of round steel tunnel, while Sir Guy and I hung on to its tail, until—

WHUMPF! We fell painlessly to the straw-covered floor beside it, in a dimly lit coop, with walls not of wood but of metal. From the lumps of rotting meat lying about and the size of the droppings scattered all around, I was quite glad I couldn't smell anything in my invisible state. The sounds of clucking and scuffling told me the horrible truth – we were surrounded by poultry-geists!

And, since we couldn't pass through metal, we were trapped.

"So far, so good, eh?" said Sir Guy.

Then the other two dead poultry-geists whizzed down the steel tube behind us and squashed us both with the scorched remains of their metal tails and claws.

"Yes, this is really nice," I mumbled.

The next moment, an electric light snapped on and a door rattled, as Mr Butt stepped into the coop.

"He'll see us!" I hissed.

"No one can see us!" Sir Guy reminded me. "Not without the scrying glasses."

"What about the other poultry-geists?" I wondered.

"BUUUUUUKKKKK!"

said one close by.

"Ah, yes! They are bred to sniff us out," Sir Guy said. "So hold still and stay undercover."

"Got it." I have never been so happy to be sat on by a dead, half-roasted chicken-devil beast.

"So!" Mr Butt's familiar voice rasped out into the room. "That's what happened to them. Dead as a dinosaur's bum, all three of them."

"Lady Jemima Smyth and her nitwit of a knight are more resourceful than I thought," came a cold and sinister voice. A voice like a spade scraping through frozen earth. I knew straight away that it could only belong to one person.

SEERBLIGHT.

Half buried in poultry-geist, I couldn't see him clearly. He was tall and thin, and seemed to shimmer somehow. His face was in shadow, but his eyes shone the palest glassy blue.

"I must capture the boy," Seerblight rasped. "His

mother, Professor Deer, holds the secret of how to make Salt of Igneous by the ton – I sense it . . . AND she is close to reversing its invisible effects. But, without persuasion, she works half-heartedly."

Mr Butt smiled. "When her loving son is in your power, she'll do the job faster . . ."

"She must," Seerblight agreed. "All has to be ready for my glorious 1000th birthday celebrations." He gave a scary, shivery laugh. "As Venus and Jupiter come into conjunction, their shared light searing the evening heavens, I shall start my second thousand years on this world . . . as its MASTER!"

"I'll get the boy for you, master," said Mr Butt, "don't you worry! I'll see the job is done! Oooooooh, yes. Just wait!"

"I will not wait long." Seerblight's voice grew its iciest yet. "Dispose of these bodies. I must return to Professor Deer and . . . encourage her."

Oh, Mum! I thought, with a shiver. I couldn't resist lifting my head to see Seerblight properly, as he turned and walked from the coop with Mr Butt.

And, as I did, I gasped. Parts of Seerblight – his left arm, his right leg, even bits of his hair – were glowing pale and translucent and just plain GHOSTLY . . . like us!

"Pow-powder," I breathed, as the hairs on the back of my neck prickled like mad. "Seerblight's been exposed to it, too!"

"What say you, lad?" Sir Guy stuck his transparent head through the poultry-geist for a better look. "*Mon Dieu!* So this is how Seerblight knew that his victims became untouchable and invisible. Half of him is going the same way. Just wait till I tell Lady Jemima!"

"First, we should follow Seerblight," I said. "He's not wearing scrying glasses, so he won't see us. And he'll lead us straight to my mum!"

"Yes!" cheered

Sir Guy. "What care we for highly dangerous magical traps left for the unwary at every turn?!"

"Er," I began. "Well, actually—"

"What caution should we show when intruding upon the fortress of the most powerful and evil sorcerer in the world?" Sir Guy boomed.

"All right, calm down!" I chewed my lip, worried for Mum, worried for me, worried for the world! And then worry turned to all-out, potentially pant-wetting panic . . .

Because the other poultry-geists had heard us, or sniffed us, or something. They were closing in, sniffing and snorting and saying "BUUUUUUUK!" in a really creepy way.

I looked up at Sir Guy. "What do we do?"

"Fight!" Sir Guy said stoutly. "Fight to the death!"

"What with?"

"Um . . . STRAW!" Sir Guy held up a small clump of wet stalks. "Ha! Yes, I think I see fear in their eyes now!"

I covered my own eyes with my hand as the poultry-geists snarled and snapped and raised their claws. "We are so doomed."

And just then, as if to confirm it, Mr Butt re-entered the coop with a large whip. **"Oi!"** He cracked his whip, and the birds about to bite us backed away. "What's got you going, you rotten, rubbish lot? Get lost, so I can reach those bodies . . ."

I thought quickly. "He can't see us, and he can't hear us, and he won't feel us if we run through him, right?"

"This is true!"

"Then *come on!*" I charged for the door, passing right through Mr Butt, and Sir Guy came after me.

And the poultry-geists came after us.

And they trampled Mr Butt into the ground as they went!

I grabbed hold of the coop door's metal handle, slammed it shut and turned the key in the lock. Mr Butt would know now he had intruders to deal with – *arrrrgh!* But at least we were outside, in a deserted yard beside the great tower (nice to know the poultry-geists were free range, huh?). It was time for a daring escape. . .

Or not.

"Oh, NO." I took in the six-metre-tall chain-link fences all around me. "They're made of metal; we can't pass through them."

"We can climb them!" Sir Guy declared. He ran up to the fence – and massive blue-and-white sparks burst through his body. Poor Sir Guy was sent flying backwards through the air – straight into *another* fence, which zapped him again. He staggered over to me and fell to the ground, eyes shut.

"Or perhaps we can't," I said.

"Intruders!" yelled Mr Butt from the coop behind us. "Get after them, you great flapping flip-wits!" ***BANG! BOOM!*** The poultry-geists were well trained, and the metal door to the coop was bulging and straining as the chicken-monsters fought to smash it down.

"Sir Guy, wake up!" I slapped his cheeks and shook him by the beard, but his eyes stayed shut. "I . . . I don't know what to do. We're totally trapped – and we're about to die!"

CHAPTER THIRTEEN

A Team is Born

(and a Book is Named!)

I knelt over the figure of this king-sized knight in his oversized underwear, listening to the coop door being bashed off its hinges, convinced I was about to be killed by a sorcerer's pet devil-chickens, when suddenly I heard something that put fresh hope in my heart.

It was a fast-approaching *"NEIGHHHHH!"*

Next moment, Maloney came leaping heroically over the high fence, snickering in the face of gravity. Of course, Jem had said that the human mind kept our feet on the ground – but clearly an everlasting horse was a different matter!

Maloney landed beside me, then stooped to lick his master's ghostly face, nudging him awake.

"You found us!" I cried. "Good boy, Maloney."

"I told you, lad," Sir Guy said groggily. "His nose can sniff out pow-powder over long distances. And, thanks to your *maman*'s work in that building, he smelled it here!"

I didn't much care how he'd found us – I loved the old horse to bits for turning up at all.

Sir Guy got back to his feet and lifted me onto Maloney – just as the poultry-geists burst their way out of the coop, Mr Butt close on their iron tail feathers.

"Away, Maloney!" Sir Guy jumped onto his horse and dug his ghostly heels into the pony's ghostly sides. "Away!"

Maloney galloped towards the fence, chased by twenty giant chicken-monsters. At the last moment, he leapt . . .

WHOOOOOSH! Over the fence we went, our cheers drowning out the angry **BUK-BUK-BUK** of our pursuers, and the raspberry blown by Mr Butt.

Maloney's jump was epic, and he landed in the shadows of the street beside the yard.

Someone stepped out in front of us – luckily, it was just Lady Jem.

"I'm so glad to find you!" She beamed up at us. "What

happened? What did you learn?"

"Maybe we could tell you back at the house?" I said, the distant *buk*king of the poultry-geists still too close for comfort.

Jem jumped up behind me onto Maloney and the pony shot away into the night.

We soon arrived back at Jem's stately home (or her *in-a*-stately home, at any rate). I marvelled again at how I wasn't out of breath, at how we'd galloped through traffic and buildings like they weren't there. It had been scary at first, just sort of passing through everything. But after a while it felt more like . . . well, like having a superpower.

I felt unstoppable!

But if only I could stop feeling unstoppable and turn normal again when I wanted to. Which was now. **Oh, Mum!** Thinking of her, alone in Seerblight's tower . . . But it sounded like she was standing up to him and not doing the work he wanted. She was tough, my mum.

"Now, then," Jem said primly in her wreck of a living room. "Tell me of your adventures. What did you learn?"

"I learned that magic fences are not very nice," offered Sir Guy.

"Neigh," said Maloney (possibly pony for "You should've hopped over it, you dummy").

I filled Lady Jemima in on all we'd overheard.

"Well, heavens to Betsy! I said that taking the elixir had left Seerblight not all there but I knew not how true my words were!" Jem gave a tinkling laugh, which she stifled when she saw Sir Guy and I were not amused. "His elixir of eternal life must have contained a tiny amount of pow-powder – stopping his flesh and bones from ageing and rotting. However, over the centuries it's nibbled away at his physical form."

"Maybe that's why he went after you and all those other pow-powdered people," I said. "To experiment on you, trying to find a way to reverse the condition?"

If Sir Guy's brains hadn't been as ghostly as the rest of him, I'm sure I'd have heard the cogs turning. "Perhaps this is so," he said at last. "Perhaps Seerblight does not wish to take over the world until he is solid again . . ."

"And he wants my mum to make tons of the stuff." I pulled a face. "That's a plan not going anywhere nice."

"At least we finally know what Seerblight wants." Jem sucked in a breath. "He wants . . . somehow . . . to take over the world."

"How original," I said. "Mind you, if he's 1000 years old now, it probably was original when he first had the idea."

Jem nodded. "I wonder which date shall mark his 1000th birthday?"

"I know not," said Sir Guy, "but he talked of a conjuring genius called Vupiter."

"He actually mentioned a conjunction of Venus and Jupiter," I said. "Whatever that is."

"A conjunction is when two celestial objects seem close together in the sky, as viewed from Earth." Jem looked worried. "It marks an auspicious time of good fortune in the old astrological calendar."

"And Seerblight's 1000th birthday happens to fall on the same day? Perfect." I sighed. "When is the next Venus and Jupiter thingy, then?"

"I shall check my computer." Jem crossed to the tattered old floor-length curtains at the broken window and slid out a chunky, retro laptop.

"Impressive," I said, unimpressed. "How do you work the keys? They're plastic, not metal."

"I don't use the keys. I operate computers from the

inside, by mental manipulation alone! And I usually piggyback on your mother's own Wi-Fi connection." The laptop seemed to switch on by itself and a search engine home page came up. "It is a difficult skill to acquire when you're an invisible apparition from Victorian times . . . unless you happen to have endless empty years stretching ahead in which to practise."

I remembered the way she'd written messages and hijacked apps on my phone and my tablet, and decided respect was due.

"Such magic is beyond me," Sir Guy lamented. "Give me instead a good sword, a strong horse and a lengthy song to sing!"

"Don't give him that," Jem said automatically. She looked grave. "It would appear . . . we do not have long. The next conjunction of Venus and Jupiter . . . is on August 27th." She looked at us. "Four days from now."

"Four days?" I echoed. "Seerblight was cutting it fine, wasn't he? Kidnapping my mum so close to his big moment."

"Her coming here – just at the right time – must have been foretold to him across the ages," said Jem. "Only by using your mother can he make his evil ambitions come true."

"And by using you, too, *mon brave*," Sir Guy added. "With you in his clutches, she'll dare not defy him!"

"Well, it sounds like someone's got to defy him," I said.

"I do not like the idea of rushing into action," said Jem.

"I DO!" said Sir Guy (surprise, surprise).

"Rushing? You've had hundreds of years to think it over . . . but now we've only got four days!" I bunched my invisible fists. "Rushing's our only chance."

"I suppose you're right," Jem agreed. "Perhaps it's time we 'invisible' individuals joined together and made a team. Got *incorporated*, you might say?"

"A team, huh?" Despite everything, I suddenly smiled. "Hey, you know what? I've got the perfect name for us . . . Invisible Inc.!"

Sir Guy looked puzzled. "You have written the perfect name in invisible ink?"

Jem shook her head. "No, no, he suggests that we *are* 'Invisible Inc.'."

"That's 'inc.' as in 'incorporated', not 'ink'," I tried to explain. "You know, like *Monsters, Inc.*—"

Sir Guy yawned noisily. "Let us move on! What is to be Invisible Inc.'s first mission?"

Jem jumped up. "I'll tell you! I'll jolly well flipping tell you! Oooh, what a mission it will be. Now we're cooking!" She stared at the laptop, wiggling her eyebrows – text began to appear in search engines and webpages loaded onto the dusty screen. "Between 1954 and 1982, I experimented with different metals. I wanted to know if some were easier to hold than others – you know, would the molecules in a copper/brass alloy be more responsive to our invisible touch than, say, marine-grade stainless steel—"

"We get you," I said quickly. "What did you find?"

"Hold on, just let me hack into this website . . ." The laptop beeped and Jem smiled. "Oooh, I'm good. Anyway, as I was saying, I did find one metal to be outstandingly responsive . . ." She blushed. "I'm rather ashamed to admit I stole a bar of it from a warehouse to run more tests."

I nodded. "And?"

"It was good!" said Sir Guy heartily. "I hit a chicken-beast with it!"

"You took the bar without permission and the wounded poultry-geist ran off with it in its beak." Jem gave him a look that suggested she hadn't forgiven him for this. "So, although my soul quails at the confession, I had to steal another bar of it."

Sir Guy beamed. "It too was good. I hit *another* chicken-beast with that one!"

"And lost it in just the same way," Jem agreed. "Well, the poultry-geists seemed to give up on us after that . . . I didn't like to keep stealing things, and computers were becoming popular so I learned about working them instead. I never got round to testing any more of that metal, but it occurs to me now that it would make a most powerful armour . . ."

"Hooray!" cried Sir Guy.

"And the name of this amazing metal?" I asked.

"What we need to find," said Jem, "is the WC!"

"You mean the water closet?" Sir Guy frowned. "The *garderobe*? The toilet? The lavatory?"

Jem was concentrating on the screen. "Aha! A window of opportunity opens for us at noon! But the WC will not be easy to get hold of. We must act as a team."

"I will!" Sir Guy assured us.

"*We* will," she said.

I nodded. And I made a quiet gulping sound. A mission! An actual, dangerous mission that would help us rescue Mum!

It's funny that Jem had just mentioned the WC. Because, if I could still use one, just then is *exactly* when I'd need to go.

CHAPTER FOURTEEN

Have you ever seen three invisible people from different times in history standing in a lay-by not far from a snack van at the side of the road with a 500-year-old pony?

Well, no, you haven't. Because they were invisible, duh.

But even if you somehow sensed their presence . . . were your three invisible people and their horse standing there because they'd hacked into the delivery website of a metal company and were planning a WC heist? In the middle of the day?

NO. Don't lie.

"I cannot help but think," said Sir Guy (and I didn't really believe him), "that robbing a horseless carriage for its WC is not entirely heroic."

"It's all in a good cause," said Jem, though she didn't look convinced.

I hoped it was. I felt bad, knowing we were about to scare

the heck out of some poor lorry driver. But, with time so tight, we couldn't afford to mess around. I looked at Jem. "Remind me again what WC stands for?"

"THE LOO!" said Sir Guy.

"Oooh, language," Jem chided him, before turning back to me. "WC is the chemical formula for tungsten carbide. Surely you must know of this chemical compound of tungsten and carbon atoms? It was invented long after my time, but was in full industrial production by the 1930s—"

"Science isn't really my thing," I admitted. "Where does the W in WC come from, then?"

"Tungsten was originally known as wolfram."

So confusing, I thought (and again: *Curse you letter W!*)

"Tungsten carbide is incredibly strong," Jem went on, "with the highest melting point of all the metallic elements. You know, the only thing harder than tungsten carbide is a diamond, so it's often used in drills and for military uses—"

Sir Guy yawned noisily. "I prefer to talk about the *real* WC."

"Well, I for one do not." Jem looked dismayed. "Noah, you live in an age of great inventions and yet you keep your water closets inside the house! Such dirt! So many germs! There beside your toothbrushes and washing implements. Ugh!"

"What's so great about outside bogs, all cold and spidery?" I retorted. "Who wants to go to the toilet outside?"

"I DO!" boomed Sir Guy. "I love it. In my day, we used a hole in the ground with a wooden seat on top. I used to sing about it."

Jem looked horrified. "Please don't—"

Too late. Sir Guy burst into song:

"Plop, plop, plop! I go
And down the chute it rushes.
Plop, ploppity-plop I go
It gives me the hot flushes!
Ploppity-plop, plop-plop-plop-plop—"

Jem cringed. "Please!" she shouted.

"Ah, non. Pees I did behind a tree."

"I said please! I find that word most offensive."

"Which word?" Sir Guy frowned. "Pees? Or tree?"

I frowned, too. "There's nothing offensive about a tree!"

"There would be if I did a poo behind it!" said Sir Guy.

Jem threw back her ghostly head: **"Can we just stop talking about poos and wees!"**

It was time to change the subject. "So," I said, "is Invisible,

Inc. ready for action or what?"

"I have my sword!" Sir Guy cried.

"I have the plan clear in my mind," said Jem.

"And I have an empty can of Fanta Orange from a bin." I held it to my mouth. "For amplifying my voice."

"Hush!" Jem hissed, with a look back at the snack van. "You will give away our presence here!"

Smoke was wafting out from the grill. I couldn't smell it, but imagined the aroma of burgers and sausages and fried onions and yum stuff like that. Of course, imagining didn't make me hungry, as I had no appetite. But my stomach shook just the same as I saw a large lorry pull into the layby towards the snack van. **Moonstick Metals and Ores** was written on the side.

"Okay, here we go!" I whispered – not that anyone visible would've heard if I'd shouted. "We'll do everything just as we agreed – agreed?"

Sir Guy looked blank. "We agreed twice?"

"Just stick to the plan," Jem told him.

The lorry rumbled to a halt, the engine was switched off and the driver – a bald, portly man with a patchy red beard – got out and headed for the snack van.

We had to act like ghosts well enough to scare both him and the snack guy as far away as possible. So I walked up behind him, took a deep breath and spoke into my can: **"WOOOOOOOOOOOOOOO!"**

The driver stopped as the metallic echo floated eerily out at him. He looked around, so I ducked behind him (I didn't want him to see the can floating in mid-air – a magician never reveals his tricks, after all!). I did it again, right in his ear: **"OOOOOOO-WOOOOOOOOOOO!"**

The driver frowned, stuck a finger in his ear, fished out some earwax and wiped it on his shirt. Then he walked up to the man in the snack van.

"All right, Wilf!" he said. "I'll have a cheeseburger and chips, and . . ."

He broke off at the sound of banging from his truck. I could see Maloney rocking it from side to side.

"Er . . . Wilf!" the driver squeaked. "You seeing that?"

But no, Wilf was not seeing that. Wilf was too busy staring as his second-best spatula rose from the draining board all by itself and started flipping his burgers for him. I took my can round the side of the van and did my loudest **"OOOOOOOOOOOOO!"** yet.

The driver opened his mouth to scream – and Jem flipped a burger into it. Wilf screamed on his behalf as his knives and forks clattered all over the floor, and leapt out over his own counter to get away, knocking down the driver. They both looked around in a panic as I **WOOOOOOOOOOOO!**d at them from behind the van. The truck was still rocking from Maloney's hooves, Jem was making as much of a metal racket as she could with the spatula and cutlery and then, as a grand finale, Sir Guy's mighty broadsword came pitching towards them, pointy end headed their way. Both of them leapt in the air and sprinted away in terror.

"Good work," said Sir Guy. "They will not be back anytime soon."

The can slipped from my numb fingers. I felt bad, seeing the mess in the snack van and the hamburgers lying on the ground. Jem used the metal spatula to turn off the grill, looking as rueful as I did. It wasn't much fun scaring people in order to steal their stuff . . .

The big knight had already crossed back to the truck to join his pony. "Let me break inside this metal carriage so you may fetch your WC." He started slashing at the back doors with his sword, denting and scraping the bodywork. "Ha! It is tough and heroic work!"

"Or we could always try turning the door handles," Jem suggested, "before another motorcar stops here in search of refreshment and wonders why a lorry stands abandoned."

"Pish. You and your reasons!" Looking a bit put out, Sir Guy stood back and let me and Jem tug at the handles. My hands slipped off them a couple of times, but, once I really concentrated, I got a grip and swung open the heavy door. There were lots of crates and boxes inside.

"While you search for your metal," said Sir Guy, "Maloney and I will clean up yonder roadside kitchen."

I approved. "That's very heroic of you."

Grinning, the underdressed knight set off with Maloney.

Jem and I got busy scanning the metal supplies inside. "What does tungsten carbide look like?"

"A grey-black lustrous solid, I believe!" Jem made this sound like the big present on Christmas morning. "Or indeed a fine dark powder."

"Look!" I pointed to two large crates in the corner of the lorry, marked WC.

"Hurrah!" Jem beamed away as she grabbed a

crowbar on a shelf and started to prise open the lid of the first crate. "There it is. Tungsten carbide! All ready to be smelted and reshaped and formed into new things."

"How are we going to get this stuff back to your place? Touching it's one thing, but carrying it . . ." I reached down to try to lift a piece of the dark material, prepared for the usual failure. But . . . **Whoa.**

The tungsten carbide was light as a feather! It weighed next to nothing. And yet I could grip it so tightly – it just felt plain and solid in my phantom hand.

"Heavens to Betsy!" Jem tried to take the stuff from me, but dropped it at once. "How intensely interesting!"

I reached in and pulled out some more blocks of tungsten carbide. It was like lifting Lego. "This stuff is amazing! It's as if I'm suddenly solid again and, like, really strong!"

Jem nodded excitedly. "Something in the tungsten carbide is peculiarly sympathetic to the rearrangement of atoms in our transmogrified bodies!"

"Huh?"

"And, since you've just turned invisible, your atoms are the freshest – that's why you're responding so well to the WC!"

That sounded kind of weird, but hey. I put down the huge hunk of metal and Jem rubbed her hands over it with enthusiasm, like a potter with clay.

"Er, what are you doing?" I asked.

"Behold!" She held up her hands – like mine, they were now coated in a fine dark dust. "A dainty dusting of tungsten carbide!" She crossed to the back of the truck, where one of those things delivery people use to wheel in big objects like fridges and washing machines stood. It had rubber handles . . . but Jem could still hold it! "Oh, YES!" she cried. "Isn't it wonderful? The tungsten carbide dust must act like an energy conductor across the transient interface. With it coating my hands, I'll be able to hold all my old scientific instruments again!" Jem did a short, formal dance. "I'm so happy, I want to hold a WC party!"

I smiled. "I'm so happy, I don't even care how wrong that sounds!"

Just then there was a massive **CRASH** and **CRUNCH.** Fearing the worst, I rushed outside – to find Sir Guy and Maloney had just pushed the snack van down a grassy slope into a tree.

"There!" Sir Guy put his ghostly hands on his equally ghostly hips. "Now no horseless carriages will come to bother us – because yon layby is all cleaned up. Who says that Sir Guy does not have the big brain, eh?"

"I can't think," I said.

"Come and join us, Guy!" called Jem from inside the lorry. "Come and join our WC party!"

Sir Guy looked worried. "You're going to love it," I assured him.

Smashed-up snack vans aside, I could hardly believe our success. One victory to Invisible Inc.!

*

We loaded the tungsten carbide on the hand trolley and wheeled it away. Of course, it was the middle of the day, which meant there were lots of people about – lots of people not expecting to find a hand trolley and two crates rolling along by themselves. We stuck to the road in the hope that people would think it was some sort of a self-propelled, automatic trolley. A couple of cars swerved or collided with lamp posts as their drivers stared in disbelief, but we made it back in the end.

Now I'm not showing off here, but I could move our haul of mega-metal more easily than anyone else, even Maloney (once we'd dusted his tail and got him to curl it round the trolley handle). I mean, we all noticed a big difference between WC and the other metals we'd tried to hold – our fingers buzzed and tingled, our invisible muscles fizzed with strength – but, freshly transformed as I was, I could push the trolley the furthest for the longest. Jem, as the next youngest, got on quite well, too – but Sir Guy, who'd been invisible for so long, found the load heavier than either of us. He didn't let this get him down, though – he just sang even louder as he pushed to make up for it:

"Though the load be heavy
And the journey long
Be glad you're not wearing
A solid steel thong!
And a barbed-wire sarong!
And shoes made from the
bottom-dwelling shark known
as the wobbegong—"

"What a lovely voice you have," said Jem shrilly, "but please, SHUT UP!"

Finally, we got back to Lady Smyth's old wreck of a mansion.

I paused at the front door. "What about the poultry-geists?" I wondered aloud. "You trashed the first ones, but won't Mr Butt send more?"

"WE SHALL BATTLE THEM ALL!" Sir Guy boomed.

"We shall *not*," Jem informed him, leading the way into the hall. "We cannot afford the distraction. Instead, we shall leave a note on the front door explaining that we have moved away to a foreign land – then hide in my super-secret, craftily-hidden laboratory and get to work."

"You have a super-secret, craftily-hidden laboratory?" I was impressed. I was less impressed by her assumption that poultry-geists could read, but I didn't mention it.

"Indeed I do." Jem smiled as she headed for the living room. "No one knows of my laboratory because it is *particularly* super-secret and craftily—"

She never finished; a noise like a siren blasted out from inside the living room. Sir Guy and I jumped and Maloney reared up, as Jem came shooting back out, flapping her arms through the air and disappearing through the wall.

"BUUUKKKKK!"

An enormous chicken-monster smashed through the doorway. It was holding a strange, chunky device in one claw – a device it pointed straight at us.

"The poultry-geists got here ahead of us," I groaned. "And this time they've got **GUNS!**"

CHAPTER FIFTEEN

Hypnotising Chickens

"Courage, *mon fils!*" Sir Guy picked up his sword. "We are untouchable. What harm can a gun do us?" He bellowed like a maniac and ran at the poultry-geist, his sword raised high above his head.

"BUUUKKKKK!"

sneered the monster, and opened fire.

Blue light flared from the nozzle and the siren noise came back – so loud it almost punched my ears out. For a moment, Sir Guy billowed like a sheet on a washing line on a windy day – and then was thrown aside as if that wind had become a hurricane. Like Jem, he was swept away through the walls, vanishing without trace.

"NEIGHHHHHHH!" Maloney was already

charging towards the poultry-geist. He reared up and brought his front hooves down on the creature's gun – thank flip it was made of metal and fell from the chicken-thing's grip. But this poultry-geist had a beak made of steel and now gripped Maloney's neck with it. A choking whinny escaped the poor pony's throat before he was tossed aside, falling through the floor in a ghostly fashion.

Suddenly I was the last Invisible standing.

The poultry-geist stooped to pick up its gun – and I shoved the hand trolley as fast and far as I could. ***WHOOSH!***

Mega-shove! The poultry-geist looked up just as the tungsten carbide crate smashed into it – and bashed its beak in. With a nasty crunch, the chicken-thing was run down flat.

I looked down at my dusty hands in wonder. "WC to the max," I breathed – let's face it, it's not the sort of thing you want anyone to overhear. Then I ran to check on Maloney, who had risen up again; he whinnied bravely and nuzzled my ghostly palm. "Is everyone all right?"

"Somewhat shaken . . ." Jem wobbled in through the front door. "But otherwise sound."

"What *was* that sound?" Sir Guy was looking wobbly, too. "I thought I would be torn apart."

"It came from the gun," I said, and picked up the fallen metal weapon.

Jem took it from me and nodded. "Since we no longer have a solid form, our atoms can be disrupted by extreme vibrations – such as very loud sound waves."

"If the vibrations were *really* extreme . . ." I gulped. "Would they kill us?"

"Oh, yes." Jem nodded gravely. "I suspect that poultry-geist assassin was sent to murder Sir Guy and me – and to kidnap you."

"Well, now we've got a ton of WC to make us tougher, right?" I looked at Jem. "I don't know what you're planning, Jem, but we've got to fight fire with fire! That was just one poultry-geist with a gun. How many will be guarding Seerblight's place when we attack? One old sword's not going to cut it."

"My sword can cut through anything!" Sir Guy protested.

"You know what I mean! We need cool gadgets like this–"

I waved the sound gun– "that make big chickens go

'GAAHHHHHH!'

We need, like, flamethrowers, acid-squirters, um . . . killer elephants!"

"Killer elephants?" Jem looked appalled.

"Whatever, you know what I mean! Armour and weapons."

"And . . . I suppose . . . we must be ready to use them in less than three and a half days!" Jem groaned. "Three and a half days!"

"I know, milady.' Sir Guy nodded sympathetically. "It is

so long to wait."

"BUUKK . . ." The bashed-in poultry-geist had woken up! It raised its head dizzily.

I shut my eyes. "Uh-oh."

"Fear not. I have an idea." Jem stepped forward, fiddling with the controls of the sound gun. "In my age, hypnotic and mesmeric phenomena were all the rage. I wonder . . ."

"BUUKKKK!" The chicken-beast was flapping weakly on the floor. Jem turned on the sound gun and a quiet, soothing OOOOOOOOH noise came out.

"You are getting sleepy," she told the poultry-geist. "You are getting *soooooo sleeeeeeeeeeeeeeeeeepy* . . ."

It roared and spat angrily from its bent beak.

"I think it is fairly well rested," called Sir Guy.

"Let me try a different pitch . . ." Jem fiddled with the gun again and this time: EEEEEEEEEEEEEEEEEEEE! A soft, sweeping hum filled the room. "Better? Are you getting sleepy NOW? I do hope so . . ."

"BUK," said the poultry-geist sleepily.

"It's working!" I encouraged her. "Keep going."

"Listen . . . and obey . . ." Jem was making her voice softer and spookier. "Tell your master there was nobody here . . . that we have gone away to live on an uncharted desert island and will not come back . . . Do you understand?"

"BUUUUUUUK . . ." said the devil-chicken dreamily.

"Then in ten seconds wake up and go!" She switched off the gun and shooed me, Sir Guy and Maloney away. "Quick, hide next door!"

We all ran through the wall as if it wasn't there, of course. Maloney snickered as we heard the poultry-geist get up, clucking in bafflement. Then a green glow showed under the doorway, before the monster floated magically away back to its hovel at the foot of Seerblight's tower.

Sir Guy looked at Jem with admiration. "A most convincing story."

"What?" I frowned. "They'll never believe it."

"Oh." Jem looked crestfallen. "You weren't convinced?"

"Well . . . no! It's got a bashed-up beak for a start – if none of us were here, how did that happen?"

"I . . . I know not." Sir Guy's voice was a hushed whisper. "'Tis a most intriguing mystery."

"No, I mean, I did it with the WC. I— Oh, never mind."

I went over to the crates of tungsten carbide. "We'll probably have a load more poultry-geists headed our way. Let's take this stuff to your secret lab."

"Maloney – keep watch!" Guy eyed me. "Is the boy allowed to know where it is?"

"Noah is one of us now. I feel we may show him."

I was moved.

Sir Guy used his sword to push away a threadbare rug from the filthy floorboards. I saw a big metal ring set into the wood – a trap door! He helped Jem lift the heavy wooden cover. Beyond it there was nothing but blackness. Jem jumped up and down in excitement, then hopped through the hatch.

CLUNK! The sound of a heavy lever sliding into place was quickly followed by the buzz and flicker of old electric lights. Jem's hidden laboratory lay revealed – an antique mess of weird scientific equipment, so covered in cobwebs and debris you'd think partying spiders had taken over and accidentally split a few atoms.

"Let's get the WC down here," she called up. "'Tis a remarkable metal, as I've said . . ." She pulled out a sheaf of papers from under a lab bench. "To pass the long,

pointless eternity of being invisible – or the last thirty years of it, at least – I sketched a few designs for possible defences. It seems that now they might come in handy."

"Designs?" I took the papers and soon my eyes were widening. "Wow! You did all this yourself?"

"I have long feared that one day Sir Guy, Maloney and myself might need to make a final fight for freedom. And if you fail to prepare . . . prepare to fail."

"Fail to prepare – HIT SOMETHING WITH YOUR SWORD!" Sir Guy boomed from up above. "I like the sound of a mighty fight for freedom. When we beat Seerblight and become the

saviours of the world, that will make us the best-ever heroes! Ever!"

"Oh, dear," sighed Jem.

"I'm not wild about battling," I admitted. "I'm just a kid. And I don't know about saving the world, but I really want to save my mum."

"Perhaps we have hidden away for too long. For all my protests, perhaps I have come to accept life as an invisible wraith . . . a ghost. Well, no more." Jem put her hands on her hips, as if posing for some invisible portrait painter. "Come, my friends. We must work hard – harder, I fear, than ever before. Let the battle for survival commence!"

CHAPTER SIXTEEN

Songs and their Dangers with Less than Three Days to Go

And so, in Jem's secret laboratory, we got busy.

Jem was in her element. And her element was chiefly tungsten (chemical symbol W, remember? Yes, this was a periodic table joke! You'll thank me when you study that in chemistry).

While she pored over her plans, deciding what to make first, the rest of us helped to transform her old Victorian boiler into a fully functional forge and furnace. With WC-dusted hooves, Maloney kicked up and trampled down the grotty old mess inside, so I could clear it out more easily. Sir Guy used his trusty old sword to cut trees into firewood, Jem added chemicals to make the flames burn hotter and soon the forge was open for business.

We needed to melt down the WC into precision tools and parts for all the incredible gadgets Jem had dreamed up. And, as she got to grips with the plans, I had a few ideas of my own for 'added extras' . . .

I'd spent enough time hanging out with Mum, watching her work, to be quite good at basic electronics. So it wasn't rocket science (well, I guess it sort of was) to work out that Jem would do all the fiddly stuff with help from me, while Sir Guy did the donkey work and Maloney did the horsey work (for obvious reasons).

I'm not going to give you a blow-by-blow account of what happened because:

a) there were a lot of blows, so I don't want you to fall asleep, and

b) I'm not entirely sure myself.

I *am* sure that I worked harder than I'd ever worked in

my life – but my invisible muscles refused to ache, and my invisible hands couldn't blister, and my invisible flesh couldn't roast in the flames of the furnace . . . It was only my mind that needed to rest, when I'd been concentrating for long stretches, and even then a five-minute catnap was enough.

I began to see why Mum, and Jem before her, had thought pow-powder a good idea: if people could only become invisible and then change back again when they wanted to – and if they owned a handy pair of WC gloves – then they could work in dangerous places, or explore deep beneath the sea, or travel long distances through extreme hot and cold, and all without hurting themselves one bit.

As day became night and night became day, we never stopped working! We couldn't. There was no time to rest. Nuh-uh. No chance.

The conjunction of Venus and Jupiter was fast approaching . . . which meant Seerblight's 1000th birthday was nearly here.

At least no more poultry-geists came looking for us. Maybe they really had believed Jem's rubbish lie. Or maybe Seerblight was preparing something nastier to come for us. My thoughts swung between wild optimism and absolute dread. It was actually a relief to have so much work to do.

Hang in there, Mum, I thought as I rewired a circuit to Jem's design. *We'll get you out. We will.*

Since I was responding best to the WC, I found myself doing most of the cutting and shaping and wiring circuits. Poor old Sir Guy was often stuck outside to guard us from poultry-geist attack. To pass the time, he and Maloney sanded and polished the metal parts that Jem and I were turning out, and chopped down more trees for firewood.

However – what he lacked in skill, Sir Guy made up for in motivational ballads, singing songs of heroic toolmanship at the top of his lungs . . .

"Oh, a man did take a spanner
And in a splendid manner
He did tighten a nut
And assemble a hut
Then broke for a well-earned banana.
So come now, ye all
And work till ye fall
Singing, Work! Work! Work! Work!
Work! Work! Work! Work! Work! Work!
Work! Work! Work! Work! Work! Work!
Work! Work! Work!
Work! Work! Work! Work! Work!
Work . . . !"

"**Arrgh!**" I looked up from the circuit I was working on. "We've got hardly any time left! How much longer is he going to sing these terrible songs?"

"He's only trying to help. I suppose." Jem sighed. "Try and ignore it."

Midnight crept close and the tuneless singing went on:

"Ohhhhhhhhh, I love my axe!
It loves me backs!
We chops up wood
We piles it in stacks.
The only way I can
relaaaaaaaaaaaaaaaaaaax
Is CHOP-CHOP-CHOP!
I got the knacks
Singing CHOP-CHOP-CHOP!
Tiddly-chop, diddly-chop
CHOP-CHOP-CHOP
all daaaaaaaaaay
CHOP-CHOP-CHOP!
Tiddly-diddly-chop,
fiddly-diddly-chop
CHOP-CHOP-CHOP in Maaaaaaay
and also other months
CHOP-CHOP-CHOP . . . !"

Jem was gritting her teeth. "I hate life."

"Maybe this will make him stop." I turned and called out to him. "Hey, Sir Guy! Can you give us something modern?"

"Modern?" came the puzzled bellow. "Modern, you say?"

"Ha! Knew that would get him!" Jem and I shook hands.

Then, to our horror, Sir Guy attempted to beatbox, medieval style (a clay drum and tabor) as Maloney joined in with some phat hoofbeats on a dustbin lid.

"Sing while you work!
Jiggle and twerk!
My knightly moves
Drive you berserk!
The way I slice and dice a tree
Is graded A and never C
B at a push maybe
If I'm not concentrating properly.
Yaahhh, take it,
M-M-M-Maloneeeey! WHEEEE.
I love to work! Work! Workeee! Work!
Work! Workeeeee! Work! Work! Work!
Work! Work! Work! Work! Work!
Workeeeeeeeee! Work! Work! Work!
Work! Work! Work! Work! Work!
C'MON! Break it down. Work! Work!
Work! Work! Workeeeeeeeee! Work!
Work! Work! Work!"

"*Noooooo!*" Jem's head struck the desk as the racket went on. "How can I manufacture the means for our survival when I no longer wish to live!"

"Sir Guy!" I yelled. "I spy a maiden in distress!"

In two seconds flat, Sir Guy dropped down through the ceiling astride Maloney, looking all about. "Where? Where?"

"Here, with her ears bleeding." Jem pointed to herself and then wagged her finger at him. "Now SHUSH!" Suddenly she slammed her circuit down on the desk. "Oh, it's no use! Using primitive tools and equipment to make high-spec technology is impossible. The armour and the gadgets – they just won't work!" She threw back her head and wailed. "THEY WON'T WORK THEY'LL FAIL AND WE'LL ALL DIE HORRIBLY IN AGONY AND SEERBLIGHT WILL CONQUER THE WORLD AND IT'S THE END OF EVERYTHING!"

There was a long silence. I didn't know what to say.

Sadly, Sir Guy thought he did. "Perhaps I could sing a motivational—"

"NO."

"You've been working really hard, Jem. Too hard," I said quietly. "But please, don't give up. My mum's a damsel in distress, too, right now – in a kind of non-wimpy, rock star way – and you've always been her heroine.

She's looked up to you her whole life."

Jem sighed. "I . . . I know, Noah. Since I googled myself, years ago, and learned that most flattering fact, I have followed your mother's career with interest."

"You googled yourself?"

"Er, maybe." Jem moved swiftly on. "I thought with your mother's excellent brain working on the pow-powder problem, Sir Guy, Maloney and I might just stand a chance of getting back to normal. So when the lodge became available to rent I sent her an anonymous email about it and left her my diary to find . . ."

"That was all down to you!" I breathed.

"I pushed her in the right direction in the hope that she might be able to cure our condition . . ." Jem looked downcast. "And, thanks to her own cleverness, she has ended up producing the finest, purest pow-powder of all for testing, in order to undo its work."

I stared at her. "So really . . ."

"Yes, Noah. I fear it is MY fault, all that has happened to her . . . and to you, too." Jem cried a single ghostly tear. "Oh, my dear boy. If my heart were still beating, I fear it would stop in shame at being the cause of so much pain and distress to your family. But . . . I . . . I simply did not mean for this to happen."

For a moment, I felt angry. But I knew that wasn't fair.

"I know you didn't, Jem." I took a deep breath. "Just like I didn't mean to run out of the house, leaving the front door open for Mr Butt to take my mum."

"And I did not mean to scare you into doing so, lad. I have ever been impulsive, eh, Maloney? Rushing in where fools fear to tread on angels . . . or something." Sir Guy sighed and patted the horse. "It seems my heroic deeds do oft-time lead to folly."

"I guess we all messed up," I said. "But hey, we've done some good stuff, too. You guys beat the poultry-geists the first time they showed . . ."

"And you sorted out the second," said Sir Guy.

"And the lorry robbery went surprisingly well, all things considered," Jem reflected. "Although we must be sure to pay back the metal company when we successfully complete our tasks."

I looked at her and smiled slowly. "When we successfully complete our tasks?"

"Yes. You are right, Noah," Jem said firmly. "We are a team."

Sir Guy smiled – then frowned. "What is a team again?"

"It's you and me and Jem and Maloney," I reminded him. "Invisible Inc. We can't give up now. We've just got to pull this off."

Jem gestured at her workbench. "But these circuits . . ."

"I know my mum's credit-card number," I revealed. (Well, I've had to buy my own baked beans on occasion.) "Is there anywhere around here that sells better circuits?"

"I . . . I believe so, yes." Jem's face was brightening. "There is a specialist electronics supplier close by – just on the outskirts of town. To get parts from there would certainly save us some time."

"Will they have what you need?"

"I think so. I have browsed its shelves many a time to soothe my troubled mind."

"Then order what you need online," I urged her, "and we'll get them to deliver . . . No, no time. Why don't I go and collect it for you while it's night time and no one's there? I know enough about electronics spares from my mum to find what we need, and Sir Guy could take over my job here for a while."

Sir Guy nodded eagerly – then grew suddenly forlorn.

"One snag," he said. "I am very sorry, but . . . if I am concentrating hard . . . I will be unable to sing."

"Sir Guy – you're hired." Jem smiled and turned to her laptop. "Now, then. No more unseemly outbursts. I'll order the parts we need!"

Relief rocketed through me.

Invisible Inc. was still in business!

*

So Jem did her online shop and emailed the list of supplies to my phone, which I collected from my house.

I felt weird standing in the quiet of the lodge. Mum wasn't a ghost – I knew that; her head was too important to Seerblight – but she still haunted the place. It should've felt like *home*, I suppose. But no. This lodge was more like a place from another time. Even the old me was never sure he belonged there. As for the invisible me? No way.

I checked the email had arrived on my poor, cracked and battered phone. It had. Weirdly, it was already open, waiting for me on the screen. She was just TOO clever, that Lady Jem . . .

So I went back to her place, where Sir Guy waited

outside with his loyal pony.

"Maloney!" Sir Guy patted him. "Are you sure you remember Lady Smyth's directions?"

Maloney reared up and waved his wire-wool hoof-mittens.

"Very well." Now he pointed to me. "Take the boy straight there . . . and guard him well!"

Sir Guy gave me a bag of tinfoil and some WC powder so I could dust my hands when I got to the shop (the better to pick out parts with), then I climbed onto the patient Maloney and off I went.

I'd never ridden a horse before, but how hard could it be?

The night was dark as we galloped, the town twinkling with lights. Seerblight's tower stood up like a crooked spear in the distance. An orange glow burned like a dying match in the uppermost window. Was Seerblight up there alone right now, plotting and planning? Where was my mum?

The electronic store was in a business park. Maloney was racing through a car park towards it when suddenly he slowed, his wire-wool hooves scrubbing at the mud.

"What is it, boy?" I asked. Then I saw the reason. Up ahead, the electronics store's front doors stood wide open – smashed apart, in fact. Parked just outside was a large, old-fashioned car like something out of those black-and-white movies you always skip channels to avoid. The interior light was on and there were people huddled inside.

No, not people.

A poultry-geist filled the front passenger seat, scrying spectacles hiding its eyes. Another was wedged in the back. And sitting there beside it was . . .

"Mum!" I breathed.

CHAPTER SEVENTEEN

On Horseback and Under Car Bottom

Mum! MUM! She was ALIVE! I knew it!

What a rush! It was her. Really her! Sitting in the back beside the poultry-geist, with her battered white Dr Dre headphones on, looking down at her lap. It was really, really her!

Wasn't it?

I suddenly grew cautious. What was this – a trap? The car had to be from Seerblight Solutions, so what was it doing parked here? Was there a really good sale on at the electronics shop? Duh! Not at this time of night!

What if Seerblight knows about Jem's invention ideas? I thought. *What if he's stealing the parts she needs so she can't make them?*

Nah, how COULD he know?

Meantime – Mum! She looked okay! She looked normal and wonderful and maybe kind of tired, but that was nothing new. Mum! I wanted to race over with Maloney, get him to kick in the door, reach inside with my tungsten-carbidey hands and pull her to safety. Only, even if the poultry-geists didn't stop us, Mum wouldn't see it was me, of course. And she'd fall straight through Maloney, too, which might be kind of a problem.

Possible plans occurred to me: I could carry her over my head, maybe? While balancing on Maloney's back?

Maybe if I took out both poultry-geists – who were so big their heads were squashed up against the car roof, sonic blasters clutched in their claws – I could get Mum to drive the car away? Assuming the keys had been left in the ignition, which they probably hadn't. And assuming the poultry-geists didn't get me, which they probably would.

As plans went, it was rubbish.

Ohhhh! MUM! If only I could contact her . . .

What was I going to do, bellow into a tin can? Jem had used my mobile phone and tablet to communicate with me, but, even if I knew how to do that, I doubted Mum would have her phone still on her, or any useful tech like that. But what she clearly DID still have were . . .

Her headphones, I realised. There was metal in those, metal I could maybe manipulate.

Could I? Did I dare?

I wondered . . . and I fretted . . .

How long before whoever had driven the car here returned from his late-night shop? Maloney was smart – I knew he understood plenty of human speech after living around them for all these centuries – but would he be able to do just what I wanted?

I had to try.

"Maloney," I whispered in the pony's ghostly ear, "here's the plan. . . "

A few moments later, Maloney charged up to the car and reared up with a neigh. Mum heard and saw nothing, of course, until the poultry-geist in the front reacted with a loud "BUKKKKKKKK!"

It pushed open the door and squeezed outside.

Maloney turned his back on the poultry-geist and wiggled his horsey butt at it in an insulting manner – just as I'd requested! The chicken-monster in the back opened its door, too – I willed it to get out and leave my mum unguarded, but no, it stayed clutching its gun and clucking malevolently. As the first poultry-geist lumbered after Maloney, and Maloney galloped away, and the second poultry-geist watched, I galloped towards the car. Of course, I couldn't pass through the door to sit beside Mum: I'd bump into the metal and the chicken-thing would get me. And, if I tried to shout at her, the chicken-thing would get me, too.

I slid underneath the car instead and closed my eyes, tried to concentrate. Mum, I thought as hard as I could, picturing her headphones, imagining the wire leading down to her ancient MP3 player. I knew how it worked because she'd bought me one at the same time, when I was small. I'd taken it apart on my eleventh birthday, trying to boost the volume. I didn't succeed – in fact, the stupid thing never worked again – but hey, we learn from our mistakes, right?

Mum! I tried to imagine my voice coming through the MP3 player, up the connecting leads and into her headphones. But nothing happened. Was I too tense? Was I just useless at this? I knew I didn't have long. I had to make this chance to speak with her count.

I just had to!

Mum, it's me! Switch off the music for a sec! I could hear the faintest tinny racket. *God, Mum, is that Def Leppard? Why? Are things really that bad?*

Still nothing, but I knew she hated it when I dissed her music. *Mum, seriously, that is, like, the least cool comeback album ever. Why don't you listen to more electro-pop like—*

"Noah!" Mum shouted.

My eyes snapped open. She'd heard me!

She called my name.

I heard a suspicious round of **BUK-BUK-BKKKKS.**

"Noah," Mum said again. "Oh, I wish I could speak to you again! I wish I knew where you were now . . ."

I'm underneath the car, Mum! But I'm invisible, obviously. I screwed up my eyes, willing the words out of my brain. *I've got some friends and we're going to come and get you out of Seerblight's tower!*

"Ouch! I'll just turn my headphones down."

I was just TOO GOOD at speaking through tiny loudspeakers from underneath an old car! If my physics teacher could see me now, maybe she'd rethink that 'Lacks application' comment, huh? Except she couldn't see me now; no one could. That was why I was here. *Mum, we're going to rescue you, as soon as we've built some things to help. We know where your lab is, but where do they put you when you're not working?*

"I'm always working there, up on the ninth floor," Mum said bitterly. "Isn't that right, chicken-monster, eh? I've had to make tons of pow-powder for Seerblight – if I didn't, he said he'd hurt my poor dear Noah . . ."

I'm okay, Mum!

"Good, because when I've finished building what Seerblight wants, he will let me go . . . That's defo safer than any other course of action anyone else could take."

I realised Mum was trying to warn me off.

He won't let you go, Mum. My brain was aching, but I kept transmitting. *Seerblight's planning something big and terrible. It must be to do with all that pow-powder – and whatever else you're making for him. What ARE you making for him?*

"You know what, chicken-monster?" Mum said quickly, as if startled. "I hope that lovely son of mine stays out of this whole business. It will all be okay. It *will*. Everything will get back to normal . . ."

Then I heard the clawing stomp of something heavy approaching the car. Peeping out past a wheel, I saw the poultry-geist coming this way, felt the car lurch overhead as it sat back inside.

"Where have you been, Big-beak?" came a rough, low voice that sent shivers through my non-existent spine. "Why did you leave the car?"

It was Mr Butt. So *he* was the one who'd been out shopping.

"**BUUUUK,**" said the poultry-geist (predictably).

"You saw that stupid pony?" He paused. "Well, well! Could it be that little Noah Deer and his invisible gang are back in town?"

I held my breath – until I remembered I didn't actually have any breath to hold. *Please don't let the poultry-geists scent me hiding under here, pleeeeeeeease . . .*

"Of course Noah hasn't come back," Mum said. "I mean, he and his friends *wouldn't* come back . . . No way."

Mr Butt seemed amused. "You don't reckon they'll try and rescue you, then?"

"They wouldn't be so stupid."

"Oh, come on. They are *pretty* stupid."

Just you wait, Butthead! I thought fiercely.

“Well, anyway, Professor Deer,” Butt went on, “guess what? Good news. I got the last components you said you needed for the job. Here, check them.”

I listened, holding my breath. *Components? What components?*

“Yes, that’s good,” said Mum faintly. “All I need to finish Seerblight’s machine is right here. Thank you.”

“Then it’s back to the tower, so you can complete the job ready for the big moment at midnight on the 27th. And, in case you had any secret hopes for a last-minute rescue by your son and his friends, I can promise you: **FORGET IT.** Because after what I’ve just done . . .”

What machine? What big moment? And what had Butt just done? His words were drowned out by the rattle and roar of the old car engine starting. Exhaust clouded right through my face, which was kind of weird – it was a good thing I couldn’t breathe or choke or I’d have been in big trouble.

Yeah. Like I wasn’t in enough of THAT already.

I forced myself to sink into the ground as the car pulled away, so none of the metal bits hanging down could get me. Then I let myself rise back up to the surface and just lay there for a few moments.

Mum . . .

She had gone again. We'd spoken and now suddenly I could think of all the things I wanted to say to her – the simple, scared-silly you-rock-Mum-please-tell-me-this-will-be-okay stuff that's so easy to forget when you're hiding under a car filled with giant deadly chickens.

Midnight on the 27th. That was our deadline to stop all this: midnight on the day after tomorrow. If Invisible Inc. had no game plan by then . . . it wouldn't matter any more.

Nothing would.

A soft neigh from the low wall beside the store told me Maloney was back. He watched me, ears pricked, head held a little to one side, then came over and nuzzled me. Man, was I grateful for the contact.

I went into the store and started picking out the things we needed. I managed to get all the little bits and pieces in my tinfoil pouch in the end, though it wasn't easy. Let me tell you, ghostly tears are a flip to blink out of your eyes.

Chapter Eighteen

Being a Most True and Worthy Account of High Adventure and Heroism by I, Sir Guy deYupp, Most Famous Swordsman in the Whole of France (Probably)

Ahhhhhhhh! Yes, thy wait is over! Here I am, Sir Guy deYupp, taking my turn to record the heroic trials of our toil and trudge. While *jeune* Noah helped Milady Jemima in the final phases of our war effort, I oversaw all other matters.

After the boy had cunningly communicated with his *mère,* we knew we must move against Seerblight on the day after tomorrow, by midnight. After that, this evil machine of his would surely be ready for its sinister work – whatever that might be. Milady Jem would have to work very fast, and so too would *mon brave,* Noah.

Ahhh, how noble it is to stand on the eve of battle! How fine the view from there, eh?

Forgive me – I am unused to writing down words, particularly with this strange metal quill. It makes me wish to record our exploits as did the monks of old. But no! For, like Milady Jemima, I can use your modern tongue! It is the piece of pie!

We threw ourselves into our labours with joy. Especially me. "PIGABUNGA!" I shouted. I shouted it often, many times an hour, loudly and at random, to give cheer to my fellows!

Verily did Milady Jemima work tirelessly, charging through her work like the finest foot soldier through the front lines of the enemy's ranks. Her designs seemed sound enough, and so too did their execution. (By execution I mean the carrying out – not the slicing off of a head! Ha ha!)

I was the appointed weapons tester, as I had most experience of fighting in the field (and in the swamp, the hillside, the beach, and ONCE even in a large tin bath! But I digress). Soon – with but a day and a half before glorious battle commenced – I was testing new weapons for the first time in 500 years!

WEAPON 1. THE SWORD OF HELLFIRE

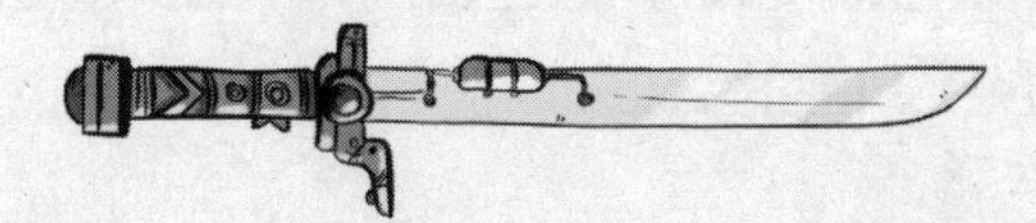

IT'S SICK! But not like someone with cholera!

I studied this weapon first with some surprise. It was made of the mighty metal, WC, and sat well in my hand.

However! I had thought a sword was felt to be too – what do you say – *primitive* for modern combat?

Not so the Sword of Hellfire!

Yes, the Sword of Hellfire (well named by *jeune* Noah) has a power pack and trigger built into the hilt and, it says here, fires a 'high-energy light ray'. I believe this is fancy speak for IT IS A SWORD-GUN THAT SMITES THINE ENEMIES DEAD AS STONES AND ROASTS THEM AS GUINEA FOWLS O'ER A FLAME! Ha ha. Result!

WEAPON 2.
THE LANCE-A-LOT

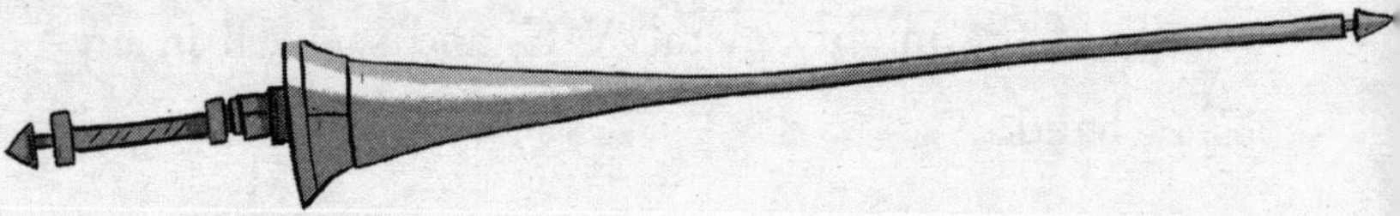

IT'S WICKED! Like a witch. And yet, do not burn it like a witch. That would profit ye not.

This lance looks and feels like an ordinary lance except the tip glows red-hot and can burn through any armour! COOL! Only, hot. Ha! Such is science.

WEAPON 3.
THE SHIELD HOLLY-CARRIER

MAX OUT YOUR FURY! This was my own design. Who needs technology! 'Tis a shield upon which I have stuck bits of very pointy holly – ouchie! Ha ha! Not only that, but the berries are poisonous! BEWARE.

*

I am also 'stoked' (like a furnace!) that my pony Maloney is armed – or, er, legged – with FETLOCK-SHOCKERS. These small battery-powered pads of WC allow him to transmit an electric shock to any who might attack him. And indeed any who might not attack him, if

Maloney so takes against him! The choice is his!

He has also been given a special BAD SADDLE. I do not mean a saddle that is very poor. This is bad in the slang meaning of the word, that it is actually not bad at all but rather good. Apparently, 'RATHER GOOD SADDLE' does not sound 'cool' enough. Although, since it is made of metal, it actually IS cool. So long as you stay out of direct sunlight.

In terms of what it does—

Oh, you will learn for yourselves. The time for battle fast approaches and I must rest. Verily, I am exhausted by this use of words. I am a warrior born, not a scribe! And so I shall take my leave of you. Do not be having the cow about this, man. Noah's report shall make good reading, I am sure. Not as good as mine, but then – ha! What COULD be, eh? Eh? HA!

PIGABUNGAAAAAAAAA!

CHAPTER NINETEEN

Super Parade!

"We're running out of time!" Jem cried, as the clock ticked towards six o'clock in the evening on our last day.

I knew it was true, but I didn't want to believe it. We'd raced and worked our invisible fingers to the invisible bones, but have YOU ever tried making sophisticated armour for four intangible people in just a couple of days?

Tick, tick, tick went that INCREDIBLY annoying clock on Jem's mantelpiece. Just under six hours left to go. Every tick was a second closer to disaster.

When the clock struck midnight – Seerblight would strike, too.

I'm not saying we were getting bent out of shape with all the tension, but . . .

I tried to stay calm. I'd been working on Maloney's Bad Saddle all afternoon, and keeping an ear out for a surprise attack from poultry-geists I felt sure would be coming, since our super-powered pony had raised Mr Butt's suspicions in the car park. The fact that it *hadn't* come wasn't much of a comfort – as we all knew the attack could come at ANY SECOND! Maloney was out on guard duty, sure . . . But, even if we **WEREN'T** attacked, we would be the ones doing the attacking! Us! Ourselves! Battling an evil sorcerer, his henchman and who-knew-what-else in his mystical stronghold that was guarded by a ton of giant devil-chickens, in the hope we could foil his plans and get my mum to safety.

ARRRRGH! **STRESSSSSSSSSSS!**

Er, anyway.

As a result of all that, I wasn't sure how Jem had been getting on.

"Okay," I said, "where are we?"

"In Milady Jemima's house!" Sir Guy declared.

I gritted my teeth. "I mean, where are we in terms of how far we've got with all the armour and weapons and stuff."

"Well." Jem sighed. "As our most experienced warriors, I have given priority to Sir Guy and Maloney—"

"HUZZAH!" Sir Guy bellowed.

"—so they are quite well covered. I have also engineered many of my own defensive creations." She cleared her ghostly throat. "But, er, as for you, Noah . . ."

I sensed this was going to be a big but. "How far have you got?"

"Well . . ." Jem looked grave.

"Let us all get into armour, so we may get used to wearing it in readiness for the battle to come." Sir Guy couldn't look more delighted, in contrast with my own terrified face. "Into armour, *mes amis!* You, too, Maloney. Come on, boy. Into armour we go!"

It was time for the weirdest fashion parade ever.

First up for inspection was Sir Guy. Jem helped him squeeze into the completed armour, while I eased Maloney into his leg-gear and his Bad Saddle which had one or two extra surprises built in . . .

"HA!" Sir Guy admired his reflection in a dusty mirror. And actually who could blame him? After so many centuries roaming in his underclothes, this biggest of knights had just over 60% of a new suit of armour tougher than anything he could have dreamed of in his own time – and far-out weapons to match.

"It is not only my atoms that are excited by this wondrous metal," he went on. "I look like a superhero! I should call myself . . . WC MAN!"

"That's, like, Toilet Man," I told him. "No one wants to be Toilet Man."

"How about War Commander?" Sir Guy held up his Sword of Hellfire and raised his voice. "As in the *comiiiiiiiiiiiics* of old!"

"Got it!" cried Sir Guy, unfazed by the shameless commercialism of the interruption. "I shall be the KNIGHT STALKER! For I stalk in the night! Dressed as a knight! Almost. And I shall talk about knights, so the KNIGHT STALKER is also the KNIGHTS TALKER! Ha ha."

"You look great," I told him.

"I feel moved to sing!" Sir Guy announced. "OHHHHHHHH . . .

Knight Stalker! Knight Stalker!
He'll cut ye down,
be ye skinny or porker!
This is your NIGHHHHHT—"

"Not now, Sir Guy!" I begged him. "Hey, check out Maloney . . ."

"Or," Sir Guy boomed, "as he shall now be known . . . Horse-o-War!"

Maloney trotted up. He looked pretty impressive, it had to be said.

"Wow," I said, impressed by the full effect. "I never saw a pony in platform shoes before."

"They give him a good height advantage." Jem had ducked behind the lab wall to get into her own outfit. "What do you think of the Fetlock-shockers?"

I went over to inspect Maloney's knees – and a massive surge of electric blue energy zapped out of them, almost engulfing me.

"They're a little bit sensitive," Jem called.

I nodded. "But totally awesome."

"yeigh!" said Maloney. Which was either the opposite of neigh, and so an agreement, or else a horsey take on 'yay'.

"And now," Jem added, "here am *I*!" The ground shook as the lab wall blew apart in a hail of rubble. Stones bounced off Sir Guy and Maloney – or Knight Stalker and Horse-o-War, if you prefer – and went straight through me.

I turned to find Jem looking, well. Kind of different.

"Well, here I am, in my protective shell of fine-strung tungsten carbide with added chemical extras." Jem shrugged and the fuzzy ball she stood in shook in sympathy. "I haven't had time to automate my defences. So I'll have to carry them behind in the wagon."

Sir Guy shook his head. "Horse-o-War will carry them for you, er . . . Superiorly-equipped Lady!"

"Who?" Jem looked appalled. "What kind of a name is that?"

"A fine name for a super-lady!" Sir Guy insisted. "Or do you prefer Baroness Boom?"

"No."

"She of the WC?"

"Certainly not."

"Woman-Woman!"

"Woman-Woman?"

"She is twice the woman you were expecting!"

"*No.*"

"Okay, maybe we pass on the super-names." I looked at Jem hopefully. "When is it my turn?"

"Er, now!" she said. "I've, um, left it on the other side of the wall for you . . ."

I hurried through the hole in the wall. Secretly, even through my growing terror at the thought of fighting, I'd been kind of excited to see what I would look like in my own suit of armour. Like Sir Guy said, kind of a superhero. A real-life Iron Man!

Or not. "I . . . don't mean to sound ungrateful," I said slowly, "but to be honest, I'm not 100 per cent happy with it."

"Nonsense, *mon brave*!" Sir Guy slapped me on the back, which set my boxes rattling. "Once we have bestowed upon you a good superhero name, you will strike fear into the hearts of your enemies! Such as . . . er . . ."

Jem bit her lip. "Umm . . ."

Maloney whickered quietly.

"Got it!" Sir Guy boomed. "Upright Metal Box Turtle!"

"What?" I cried. "That's the worst name ever."

Jem laughed weakly. "Names aren't everything. I know it doesn't look very, er, polished. But it is still a most sturdy suit of armour."

"Quite so, milady!" Sir Guy shouted. "And now we dare tarry no longer. There is a damsel to save and a world to rescue – or maybe that is the other way round? A damsel to world and a rescue to . . . No." He shook his head. "ANYWAY! Let us swiftly test what weapons we can and then . . . LET BATTLE BEGIN!"

CHAPTER TWENTY

Battle DOES Begin!

It's not easy to sneak a big metal wagon full of fantastic armour and weapons through the middle of town, no matter how invisible you are. And we couldn't wait for it to be properly dark, or we'd have just three hours or so left before Seerblight hit the big 1000. Who knew how long it took to do battle with an evil sorcerer? But we kind of felt that three hours would be cutting it fine.

Then again, in my lousy, unfinished, ultra-basic suit of armour, I would feel lucky to last three *minutes.*

We knew that people would end up staring at a wagon

rolling itself along, so Sir Guy went out and found a scarecrow and impaled it on his sword. Then we brought it back here and got an old cloak on it. All I had to do then was sit invisibly in the metal wagon with Jem on one side and Sir Guy on the other, holding the scarecrow in front of me with the metal end of a pitchfork. We hitched the wagon to Maloney and off to town we went, on a route calculated by Jem to be the quickest and quietest. The overall effect was that of a sinister hooded figure pulling a wagon full of scrap through the gloomiest side streets in town while making horsey clip-clop noises – with a large fork in his back. Perfect!

Mostly, people just stared or ran away rather than calling the police or something. It was a pretty tense time, though, the whole of Invisible Inc. rolling ever closer to Seerblight's tower. I felt horribly nervous. Sir Guy was smiling. Jem looked close to tears. I wondered what Maloney was thinking.

Seerblight's tower loomed high over the town. I looked up at it and shivered. So much depended on the next few hours.

At last, we reached that creepy, horrible place. It was

eight o'clock.

Four hours to go.

I eyed the metal shutters that shielded the ground-floor windows from view, as Maloney pulled up in a quiet side street. It was weird to think that Sir Guy and I had already been inside . . . and horrible to think of the stinky, horrible coops full of poultry-geists on the other side . . .

"Well! Guess it's time to put on armour, everyone," I said. We hadn't worn it on the way here because people would've seen us – and I might have caused a couple of people to die laughing. I willed myself to float down to the pavement. "Come on, then . . ."

"Hooray!" cheered Sir Guy, grabbing his armour from the back of the cart and racing down the alley to change.

Jem looked nervous. "Er, Noah? I feel so dismayed that you must wear crude armour with no electronic defences. Why not wear my armour and take all my gadgets, while I wait for you outside?"

I stared at her. "Are you saying you want to bail on the mission?"

"I'm a scientist, not a superhero!" Jem sighed,

shamefaced. "Unless 'She of the WC' refers to the fact that, were I human once again, the toilet would be reeling under the ferocity of my onslaught right now."

"Hey!" I blinked. "That was never a toilet joke, was it?"

"If you can't beat them, join them."

"Listen, Jem. You helped me so much when I joined you. You've been amazing, from start to finish." I placed my hand on her arm. "You tried to help me and Mum, before Mr Butt came to get us. You've tried to kit us all out with amazing gadgets and defences . . ."

"Tried, tried, tried, yes," Jem snapped. "But never once have I succeeded."

"Well, this time we're all here to work together. Perhaps that's the way we'll succeed – and join the real world again." I nodded to Seerblight's tower. "Plus, anyway, FYI – I really, really want to wear my own armour after you obviously went to SOOOO much trouble perfecting it for me."

"Why, you cheeky scamp! Be glad you have any armour at all!" Jem smiled despite herself, straightened her invisible shoulders. "Well! Statistically, I suppose I should succeed in some venture sooner or later. And this time, if not sooner . . . there will be no later." She patted my hand. "Forgive my cowardice, Noah. I shall don my armour and try my best, of course."

"Of course you shall!" Sir Guy had changed into his own WC armour and was now placing Maloney's Fetlock-shockers in position. "Before this day is out, a great victory shall be won!"

"And hopefully not by Seerblight," I murmured. As Jem got changed, I slipped on my metal boxes. They weren't exactly snug or sleek, but hey! They were strong and weighed almost nothing at all.

"We will win no awards for style, I fear . . ." Jem, now looking something like a massive metal hedgehog on a half-ton of caffeine, smiled at me. "But perhaps if we are extraordinarily, ridiculously lucky . . ."

I nodded. "Because we totally have been up until now."

"We shall triumph, *mes amis*. We must!" Sir Guy fitted the Bad Saddle onto Maloney's back, then swung himself onto it. "Now! There are ten floors in Seerblight's tower all together, *non*? And the lad's *maman* says she is being held on the ninth. So that is where we must go."

"Shame we can't find a really, really long ladder and climb straight there," I said. "These ground-floor shutters look pretty tough. They won't be easy to get past . . ."

"But at least we shall have the element of surprise," Sir Guy announced. "Because Maloney and I shall NOT enter through the ground floor. We shall enter through the window on the THIRD floor instead! Ready, Maloney?"

"YEIGHHHH!" whickered the pony.

Sir Guy held up the Sword of Hellfire. "Then let us away! LAUNCH THE BOUNCERS"

And suddenly – **BOIINNNNNG!!!** – enormous springs popped out from Maloney's platform hooves – that's what was packed inside! The knight and his steed went shooting through the air towards the third-floor window. Sir Guy fired his sword and – **KANNNNNNNNG-GANNNK-TISSSSH!!!** – in a blaze of purple light, the glass shattered.

Horse and rider had made it inside!

Straight away, I could hear shouting and thumping and

things breaking from up on the third floor. "Is Sir Guy in trouble, d'you think?"

"Don't worry." Jem was busy stuffing her haul of chemist's equipment into hidden compartments within her grey, metal, swirly armour coating. "To me, it sounds like he's having fun!"

I half smiled. "And while Sir Guy and Maloney are distracting Seerblight's defences up there . . ."

"It's time that we broke in at ground level." Jem looked down at the last remaining jars and beakers in the wagon. "As the youngest, strongest one of us, would you mind pushing this cart up against the wall?"

"Not a bit." My hands were thickly coated with WC dust (which still sounds 'ewwwww', but you know) so I took hold of the wagon and pushed it up against the great metal shutters.

Jem lit a match, dropped it inside and . . .

SHA-BOOOOOOOOM!

The entire wagon exploded with the force of . . . of . . . of something you've never heard of before because it was so epically awesome it somehow transcended your ability to compare things and went straight to the "WHOA,

MOMMA!" centre of your brain.

I was terrified at first: *Fire! Shock waves! Smoke!* Fatal Catastrophe Central! But soon I realised that although my armoured boxes rocked with the force of the blast, the heat of the flames never reached my invisible skin. And the black smoke belching out from the building never bothered me; it didn't sting my invisible eyes or catch in my invisible lungs.

"Whoa, Momma!" I said. "Jem, what did you do?"

"I lined the wagon with a highly explosive chemical compound – and behold! An entrance has appeared!" She gestured to the thick black smoking wound in the wall. "I suppose . . . we should go inside?"

I wanted to agree, but the words had thrown fiery arrows at the back of my throat and they could only stick there in silence. I knew my mum was up in this sinister building somewhere. So were Sir Guy and Maloney, and so were who-knew-how-many horrors, lying in wait to get us.

But hiding down here wouldn't help matters.

Invisible Inc. had to meet this stuff head-on – and deal

with it.

With a yell of "ATTACKKKKKK!", Jem and I charged through the terrible curtain of smoke and flame and ran inside.

CHAPTER TWENTY-ONE

Danger and Traps Aplenty on the Ground Floor: Going Up?

"One thing surprises me!" I shouted at Jem. "Breaking in like that, I'm surprised we didn't set off any alarms—"

BLARRRRRRRRRRRRRRRRR!!!

The alarms sounded like souls screaming in torment. And they weren't the only ones. The noise was deafening, sound waves so intense it was like the air had turned to knives, ripping at my invisible body. I saw my form wobbling out from under my boxy armour, just as Sir Guy's had billowed like old laundry back at Jem's house.

Jem was better protected inside her crazy spiky ball, but still clutched at her ears. "We must turn off that alarm!"

"No kidding," I yelled. "It'll bring every poultry-geist in the building coming here faster than a—"

"BUUKKK-KKKKKK!"

The sound of a dozen giant killer-chickens added layers of horror to the din as a mob of poultry-geists came crowding towards us through the smoky corridor.

I would've frozen in horror, but my invisible form was too busy spiking and shifting with the noise. But Jem reached beneath her tangled suit of armour, raking at her armpit.

"Aha! Found the button." She looked at me. "Here goes."

"Here goes what? Our lives?"

"One of my bright ideas. Hide your eyes!"

"Uh-oh." I looked away as Jem pressed the button inside her suit . . .

And lit up like a miniature sun!

Blinding ultra-white, the searing incandescence boiled the smoke away and seared the sight of the poultry-geists as they came towards us. Their scrying specs cracked and shattered, their steel-tipped wings came up to cover their eyes, but too late. The glare was so great that their plucked pink skins began to sizzle and smoke. Clucking in angry panic, they blundered past us, blowing on each other, fanning each other, smashing into walls, tripping over each other, starting a poultry-geist pile-up. Jem pushed me ahead of her as we ran on down the corridor in the direction they'd come from.

"Most satisfactory," Jem yelled to me over the din of

the alarm. "You see, I coated the surface of my suit in auto-ignite magnesium with glo-faster stripes. For anyone who is not invisible in close proximity, I imagine the experience was most unpleasant."

"Shame your magnesium couldn't melt the sirens!" I shouted back.

We quickly reached a door in the wall marked STAIRWELL. "Let's see if it's any quieter on the floor above!" Jem threw it open and ran inside – then jerked to a horrified halt, arms windmilling wildly.

She was about to tumble down a huge, circular hole!

"Nooooo!" I tugged her back just in time and we fell to the floor together.

"Whoa," I said. "That stairwell is more well than stair . . ."

"So I observe," said Jem. "A trap for the unwary."

I couldn't think for the din, and the sonic vibrations tugged at my pale, glowing skin, which looked to be growing baggier with every second. "We've got to do something about that alarm . . ."

"Keep running!" She lumbered onwards in her WC suit like a spikily armoured elephant. "Perhaps we'll find its source."

We came to another wooden door marked STAIRWELL on our left. I opened it hopefully – and a huge poultry-geist, almost twice the size of the others, burst out from inside. I squealed in alarm, threw myself back— Just as Jem sent a bright blue spray squirting out from a concealed nozzle in her suit, like a sprinkler – aimed directly at the creature's eyes.

"BUKKKK-ARRGH!" The monster yelled and flapped its wings so much it actually rose up into the air and slammed its head on the ceiling. As it crashed down again in an unconscious heap, the alarm stopped dead.

I turned to Jem. "That thing must have been controlling the alarm!" I realised, my words loud in the unexpected hush. "What was in that spray?"

"I have no idea," Jem told me. "But I think it stings."

I stared down at the unconscious brute of a beast in a silence that seemed somehow scarier than the sirens.

"Well, I reckon we must've found the real stairwell this time, anyway." I peered into the darkness beyond. "Or why leave a big old poultry-geist to guard it?"

Jem nodded. "We must get upstairs and join Sir Guy and Maloney – once we've made certain it is safe."

"Safe . . ." I'd noticed a strange pattern of lights pulsing inside the darkness. "Safe! Of course it's safe!" The lights were throbbing rhythmically . . .

Almost . . . hypnotically . . .

"Goodness." Jem had straightened up. "This light display is most beautiful, is it not?"

"It is," I agreed, rising myself and walking slowly closer to see. "Really beautiful . . ." The lights were so pretty in the now-silent darkness. Like an enormous eye, staring at me . . . staring into my soul . . . commanding me and Jem to come closer . . . closer . . .

Oblivious to sinister puns, drawn by the beauty in the eye that we beheld, we came closer . . .

closer . . .

CLOSER . . .

CLOSER . . .

But, just as we reached the final step—

STARE WELL

CRRRRA-KOOOOOOOM!

The noise and tremors of Sir Guy and Maloney's incredible dramatic entrance distracted me for a moment. "Safe? No! It . . . it ISN'T safe." I shook my intangible head, concentrating hard. "Not one bit!"

Finally jarred free from the *stare*well's hypnotic effect, I saw that, far from wandering in a wonderland of colourful beauty forever more, I was ACTUALLY about to step into blazing-hot volcanic lava!

And so was Jem . . .

"No! Get back!" I grabbed hold of Jem's arm and yanked her away with all my strength. She stumbled and fell on her armoured butt. Then I kicked the door shut.

"Oof!" Jem stared around in confusion. "What happened?"

"Sir Guy and Maloney saved us! Well, they accidentally fell through the ceiling, anyway." I ran over to check on them, sprawled on the floor. "Are you all right?" I asked Sir Guy as he pulled his lance out from underneath him. "What happened to you on the third floor?"

Maloney neighed, kind of indignantly. I realise he's the only one of Invisible Inc. who hasn't had his own chapter, so here – I've let him fill us in on his own ordeals with his master. (Or try to fill us in. He is a horse, after all.)

Crash through window we did. Whump! Neigh! Big chicken – boom!

WHERE IS THE GRASS OF MY YOUTH?

"Come, fine horse," says master. "Let us rejoin our friends and help them!"

(ONCE THERE WAS A FIELD! I saw a flag.)

Down the stairs go we. Most horses cannot go down the stairs!

(continued . . .)

ME SPECIAL HORSE — SUGAR LUMP WORTHY!!

Why is the special room on fire?

Horseshoe! Horseshoe.
HORSESHOE!

I have four! GOOOOOD.

What happened to floor?

I am on new floor!

Why are I upside on the down?

GRASS ONCE WAS NICE
I miss the stables of youth.
NEIGH!

"Well, thanks for filling us in, Maloney," I lied. "Sir Guy, can he lead us up to the pow-powder? If my mum's been working on it . . ."

"Of course!" Sir Guy did an air pump with his hand. "We took a staircase down from the third floor to the second and the first – but it must continue down to here, too, must it not?"

"Sounds likely," I agreed.

"It will be round about in . . ." Sir Guy pointed his Lance-a-Lot behind him. "This direction! Come!"

"Very well." Jem was staring into the lava as if unable to believe how close we'd come to stepping into it. The WC we wore would have sunk into the molten magma, trapping us there – until something horrid sent by Seerblight got us, no doubt.

Something that might very well already be on the way . . .

Jem stayed crouched over the lava, holding her hand over it. "Come *on*!" I pulled her back, she quickly adjusted her armour, and we all followed Maloney down the corridor, as he sniffed out the way.

Around the corner, he came to an unmarked door.

And, sneakily, THIS was the stairwell, unadvertised, hidden in plain sight. Sir Guy yelled and led a charge up the steps – until we all shushed him and suggested a lower-volume-based approach might be a good plan.

We ran up past the doorways to the first floor . . .

The second floor . . .

The third floor . . .

It was all going so well!

Too well.

For, as we approached the fourth floor, the door to the stairwell swung open and a familiar burly figure with a bum-cleft in his chin stepped into view. His eyes stared out in different directions. His grin was yellow and crooked. Fear prickled at my invisible skin.

Here, to face us, was Mr Butt.

CHAPTER TWENTY-TWO

The Heat of Buttle

"So. There you are!" he said. "Well, you've done pretty well to get as far as you have."

"Of course we have!" Sir Guy agreed. "And we shall get far enough to topple your vile master, mark my words!"

"Seerblight works at the top of his tower." Mr Butt stepped out onto the concrete landing. "He is preparing for his great moment, but it is a moment you shall not live long enough to witness."

"We'll see about that," said Jem, pushing forward. "Come along, everyone! He is only one man and unarmed."

"Unarmed, perhaps . . ." The boss-eyed weirdo smiled.

"But not . . . un**BUTTED**."

"Huh?" I said.

"NNNNNNNNNN!"

Mr Butt bent his legs and strained, as if to demonstrate his butt in the worst possible way. But no. Something was happening.

Mr Butt was changing. Massive muscles twitched around his arms and chest, and his shirt tore open like the Hulk's. But— No! No, those weren't muscles after all.

They were butts.

Mr Butt had transformed into a much larger creature, with weird bums growing all over him. I stared in horror, and my friends did the same, as each set of chilling cheeks opened and closed like a wobbly mouth. But Mr Butt had saved the worst for last. He turned his back to us, hunched over – and the last remains of his shirt ripped away to reveal a bottom-crack that ran the entire length of his back.

"The ultimate 'builder's bum'," I muttered.

"So, tell me . . ." Mr Butt turned back to face us, and I saw that even his cheeks had grown more buttock-like, pushing his features into a dark cleft in the middle of his face. **"Now that you have gazed upon my many butts, do you not fear me?"**

"I think you're a loony," I said, as Jem and Sir Guy agreed and Maloney nodded his head.

"And I believe, Monsieur Loony. . . it is time to kick butt!" Sir Guy led the attack, swinging his Sword of Hellfire above his head. **ZZZZZPP!** He fired fierce torrents of laser energy straight at Mr Butt . . .

But the bottom-man simply laughed. The energy was drawn inside his tush-covered torso and disappeared.

Changing tactics, Sir Guy charged at the weirdo – only to bounce straight off his many-bummed physique and slam into a wall.

Desperately, Maloney galloped up the stairs and tried to push Mr Butt over with his powerful hooves – but the horrible henchman raised his right arm and the row of bums growing there clamped down on the pony's tail like a foul, fleshy hairclip. In a show of supernatural strength, they hurled him aside to land on Sir Guy.

Angrily, I found myself leaping to the attack, too. But, before I could bring my boxed fists to bear, the multiple bottoms in Mr Butt's chest blew off as one, creating wind that was more like a force-ten gale. My armour was sent somersaulting away, and I went with it, limbs flailing, totally out of control. I landed on top of Maloney, on top of Sir Guy, and all three of us went tumbling down the steps. I was just grateful I couldn't smell anything – and even more grateful when Jem crouched beside us and helped me up.

"Come on, then!" Mr Butt snarled. "Fight me! One at a time or all together, I don't care!"

"I think we've just proved that brute force and *butt* force don't mix," Jem murmured. "We need to use our heads."

"I am not letting *my* head get anywhere near those bums!" I said. "The question is – why is he doing this? I mean, if he wanted to stop us in our tracks, all he has to do is threaten my mum."

Jem nodded worriedly. "It's almost as if he's trying to test us in some way."

"Then let us end the test now!" cried Sir Guy.

"I've got an idea," I said. "Sir Guy, how hot does your Lance-a-Lot get?"

"Hot enough to be red," he confirmed.

"Then crank up the power," I murmured. "This battle's about to ignite!"

I climbed the steps and ran once more at Mr Butt, head down in my primitive armour to charge him as hard as I could. But this time Mr Butt turned his gruesome, bared back-butt to me and let fly with a hideous wind-ripper that must have broken records. I was almost blown away again, but just managed to hold my ground.

"Now, Sir Guy!" Jem shouted. "Do it now!"

Sir Guy hurled his Lance-a-Lot – and, as the super-heated tip neared Mr Butt, the dark fart caught fire! The blaze whooshed backwards, following the gas trail to its foul source in a split second.

"AIEEEEEEEEEEE!" Mr Butt's yell echoed off the concrete walls as he exploded in an all-consuming fireball. I closed my eyes. My armour rattled. I imagined the horrible heat.

I'm not sure how long I kept my eyes closed. But, when I opened them again, the flames had faded . . . and there was nothing left.

"Your plan worked well," said Sir Guy approvingly.

For a moment, my confidence soared. Then I just felt sick. "I . . . I didn't think it would kill him."

"'Twas working for Seerblight that killed him," Jem said

softly. "Well, and you a little bit, I suppose."

"Do not be sad, *mon ami.* Victory is ours!" Sir Guy cheered, as Maloney neighed. "We came out on top – and the bottoms came bottom!"

"Come now," said Jem. "Let us reach the ninth floor and dear Trudi Deer – before climbing to the top floor . . . and facing Seerblight for the final time!"

CHAPTER TWENTY-THREE

At Last, the Lair of Seerblight

I followed Sir Guy and Maloney as they clattered up the concrete stairs in their fine armour. Jem was right beside me. Invisible Inc., somehow still all together, still going, still ready to do whatever they had to.

So many steps – but nothing else in our way. Was Seerblight too arrogant to believe that intruders would get this far . . . or were we running into the most terrible trap ever?

My intangible heart was still not beating, but I felt super-scared. What would we find at the top of the tower?

It was what we found on the staircase on the seventh

floor that baffled us. The steps were covered in cute, fluffy rodents like hamsters and mice, and the air was thick with tweeting little birds flapping all about.

"Since brute-force techniques have failed, Seerblight is trying something sneakier." Jem sighed. "An impenetrable layer of enchanted cuteness."

I tried to pick up some of the hamsters, but they squirmed and wriggled in my grip. "Their fur!" I realised, quickly releasing them. "It's wiping off my WC dust!"

"Why, the wily old stoat!" Jem hissed.

Sir Guy groaned. "There is a stoat also?"

"I meant Seerblight! It's as if he's been watching us and now is tailoring his attack to exploit our weaknesses."

"And he is right." Sir Guy clapped a hand to his face in despair. "The only way forward is to trample these blessed little animals. We cannot go on!"

"We must!" I told him. "We've come too far to be stopped now."

Jem pulled an orange hose from inside her spiky suit and considered it. "I suppose I could gas them all with a toxic agent?"

I frowned. "Stay calm!"

"Very well, a concentrated blast of air, then," she suggested. "I can create a kind of bird-free corridor in the air."

"Much better. But there's still the mice and hamsters . . ."

Jem produced a large metal mallet from a concealed back pocket and weighed it thoughtfully.

"No!" I looked at Maloney. "Do you think you could jump over them, boy?"

"Of course!" Sir Guy beamed. "He can and so too may we! We do not have springs in platform hooves as Maloney does, but his Bad Saddle is in fact an *excellent* saddle. For within it Jem has hidden an EJECTOR SEAT."

"I have," Jem confirmed. "Well, you never know when a horse might need to jettison its rider at high speed."

Hope of continuing our quest seized that unbeating heart of mine. My mum must be SO CLOSE now! "I'll go first," I said quickly, scrambling into the saddle. "Ready with the air blast, Jem? Ready, boy?"

Jem held out her orange hose. **WHOOSH!**

"YEIGGGH!" cried Maloney. **BOINGG!** His saddle burst open and I was sent hurtling through the air to end up on the concrete landing of the eighth floor. So close now!

Sir Guy followed after me, catapulted like a knightly rocket from the saddle, and Jem came next, still wielding her air-blowing hose. She kept a path clear for Maloney, his platform launchers overcoming the rush of air blown against him.

"Brilliant!" I was already climbing up the steps from level eight to level nine. "We're nearly there! Keep going! We must keep going!"

A few metres more and there it was. Finally. The door to level nine, where my mum's laboratory could be found.

And my mum?

And Seerblight?

And nameless horrors lurking in every corner?

And so on??

Sir Guy might have noticed my face (or more likely was just enjoying himself). "Milady and I will go in first, lad," he told me.

"Oh, good," said Jem unhappily.

"While we attack all enemies in our way, you must go on a mission of liberation and set free your *mère*!" Sir Guy put a hand on my shoulder. "You are up to this challenge, yes?"

"I've got to be," I murmured. Maloney nuzzled his head against me. Well, he nuzzled his heavily armoured head against my chest box, which wasn't quite the same thing. But I appreciated the gesture.

With a heroic whinny, Maloney reared up and placed his hydraulic hooves against the door. At the same time, his head armour lit up bright red and some kind of laser beam went flashing out from his forehead. The door was blown apart and Maloney strutted through, with Sir Guy wielding his sword and lance in different hands and Jem following on behind with Bunsen-burner shoulder pads sending hissing blue flames out into the gloomy corridor beyond. For a moment, then, scared as I was, I felt a real pride, too – to know that these were my friends, and that they would fight till the end alongside me.

Although 'the end' could not be far away now. Midnight must be fast approaching . . .

A few moments later, a horde of men in black dressing gowns came jumping and high-kicking into view. I held still, wary and afraid. Either these were members of some strange bedtime cult or they were martial arts experts. And – oh, NOOOOOO – they were all armed with sound guns.

As one, they opened fire, and the air was soon filled with the insane honk and hoot of their blasts. I tried to force a path through them, as highly-trained fists rained down blows that would break bone on my armour, jolting me this way and that so that I staggered, gritting my ghostly teeth as my movements got less co-ordinated. **PWARRRRRRP!** One of the guns was jammed up against my helmet; when the trigger was pulled, it almost knocked my head off with a barrage of ear-splitting sound.

I thumped the man away with a WC headbutt, sent him reeling towards Maloney, who zapped him with his Fetlock-shockers. Sir Guy was bellowing as he smashed heads together, and Jem maintained her calm as her suit catapulted test tubes full of explosive powder through the air.

Then I heard a call, distantly through the rage of battle: **"Noahhhhhhh!"**

"Mum!" I breathed.

And, while my friends battled on and kept the martial artists busy, I managed to push and shove my way through the ranks blocking the corridor. Fists and sound guns were shoved in my way, but I knocked them aside, faster, harder. I kept on going. I wasn't about to let anything stop me now.

BE A FINE ARTIST,
DAD SAID. BE A PORTRAIT
ARTIST. BUT NO, I HAD TO BE
A MARTIAL ARTIST,
DIDN'T I?

Not now that I was so, so close . . .

Finally, I fought my way through to the other side and pounded along the corridor, my head ringing, desperate to find—

"Mum!" There she was, the other side of a thick glass partition and a lab bench covered in electronic wiring, bric-a-brac – and the good old, bad old the **BRIAN**™ Scan-and-Zapper.

A fierce, brawny ninja stood at her shoulder – and now grabbed her in a necklock.

"Hey!" I shouted. "Let her go!"

As if she hadn't noticed the necklock, Mum stared at me, face fixed in amazement – and hope.

I gazed out at her, through the eyeholes in my helmet – and remembered that my armour was the only part of me she could see.

The ninja looked at me, his face twisted in hatred.

Then his face was twisted by my mum's elbow, as with a yell of anger she broke his hold, spun on her heel and clobbered him in the face. He slammed against a rack of electronics behind them and, as he bounced off it, Mum chopped him hard with the side of her hand on the back of the neck. The ninja crashed against her desk and slid weakly to the floor.

I didn't wait to watch. I was already hammering at the lab door with my WC fists! The entire glassy wall shattered under my attack; suddenly Mum's lab was open-plan, as one with the corridor. "Mum!" I rushed inside. "MUMMM! You're all right! And you were brilliant just then!"

The WC helmet amplified my invisible voice, of course, like talking into a can only way stronger and better. Mum actually heard me! "Noah!" She had tears in her eyes. "Oh, Noah, is it really you?"

Then a voice came from behind me; a voice like the purr of the oldest, coldest tiger alive – a vampire tiger who lived in a freezer on a steady diet of puppies, kittens and mice "Oh, yes," the voice said. "Yes. It is him . . ."

I turned as you do in a nightmare, invisible hairs rising on my invisible neck. There he stood in the middle of the plain grey corridor, deepening the shadows around him. Seerblight.

I'd heard tell of him from Jem and Sir Guy, I'd glimpsed him and heard him speak back in the chicken hovel . . . He'd

38

Seerblight in his villainous majesty. Speech bubble: How do you DOOM?

been frightening enough then, but now he was here the effect was doubled, tripled. Just his eyes alone – his wide blue eyes in the lined, sallow face – you could tell he had seen things no human ever had, and done things no human had ever done. His hands gleamed, encased in metal gauntlets, while his arms glowed eerily, half invisible. The smile he showed me was like the scurrying of rats across a shadowy floor. He looked, well, totally BRRRRR-RRRRRR.

"Noah," Mum said quietly, "just remember, love, he still goes to the toilet like the rest of us!"

This injection of normality brought me back to life. I tore my gaze from Seerblight, saw the **BRIAN**™ on the table. With impressive action-hero reflexes, I lunged for it, picked it up, aimed and fired the scan ray at Seerblight. It hummed and a thin beam of red shone over him.

"Ha!" I shouted. "Now I've scanned you. Don't move a muscle or I'll zap you with pow-powder, Seerblight! You'll go fully invisible and then . . . and . . . then . . ." I glanced at Mum, but there was no triumph on her face. "Er . . ."

"Oh! Look. I'm moving a muscle, Noah Deer." Seerblight took a menacing step towards me, his hands outstretched. "Aren't you going to open fire?"

Frankly, yes, I was. I aimed carefully – although with him right in front of me, it would be difficult for me to miss – and squeezed the trigger again.

But nothing happened.

Seerblight laughed.

"Oh, no . . ." I pulled and pulled the trigger. It refused to respond. "No, no, no, NO! Come on!" I shouted at the **BRIAN™**. "You've got to work!"

"It's disconnected, Noah," Mum said quietly. "The scanner still works, but the pow-powder zapper part of the original mechanism has been taken out . . . and put somewhere else."

"Indeed it has." Seerblight brought up a withered hand and knocked the **BRIAN™** from my grip with surprising strength; it went skittering across the floor. Then Seerblight gripped my wrist, metal gauntlets crushing my flesh like the devil's own pliers. As my Mum yelled, "**NOOOOOO!**", the old man loomed over me like some horrible vampire, the sharp points of his teeth bared in a gloating smile.

CHAPTER TWENTY-FOUR

Vile-and-Terrible-Evil-Plans-R-Us-a-Go-Go

Mum hurled herself across the lab bench and with an angry shout shoved Seerblight away. He staggered back, regained his balance, fixed Mum with a glare so malevolent it would make ravens explode. She clutched her head, then slumped to the floor.

"What did you do?" I cried, voice cracking.

"I will not tolerate interference from my slaves," said Seerblight. "She will recover, boy. Indeed, she will live forever . . ." He chuckled, a hateful, frozen chugging of old organs.

But the laughter was drowned out by a pounding, clomping clamour from the main corridor. It distracted the evil old techno-wizard, halted his horrid advance.

"Ha! Jem and Sir Guy and Maloney!" I shouted. "They've beaten your ninjas and now they'll get you!"

I wanted to see fear on the ancient, wizened face – but only a sinister smile sat there. "Yes, I have been watching you and your friends. You have acquitted yourselves well," he declared. "Even defeating my Head of Operations, Mr Butt."

I saw that Jem was leading the charge towards Seerblight, with Maloney and Sir Guy close behind. Yes! My fellow Invisible Inc.-ers were back on the scene!

"Noah," Jem cried. "Are you all right?"

"He still stands!" said Sir Guy. "While those ninja fools will be lying down in their dressing gowns, sleeping for a long, long time . . ."

"Well, well." Seerblight remained still, cloaked in gloom as if the light still shied away from him. "I am impressed." Not even the dust and debris dared to go too near his horrid form.

"At last, foul varlet." Sir Guy raised his lance at Seerblight. "We have you in—" He gasped, his body stiffening. "Have you . . . in our . . . power?"

Jem was suddenly rooted to the spot, staring down at her metal boots, pressing at her many hidden buttons, but finding none of them. "What is happening? My gadgets are not responding!"

"NEIGHHH!" said Maloney, who had frozen stiffer than any of us.

"Of course they are not!" Seerblight crowed. "Because . . . I CONTROL YOUR ARMOUR!"

I tried to move myself – just a jerk of the arm – and quickly realised that my own 'frozenness' was down to my being petrified, not some mechanical fault in my armour. There were no mechanics in it that could go wrong, since Jem had run out of time before she could make them.

But it struck me suddenly – Seerblight wouldn't know my armour was unenhanced. He hadn't noticed my little wobble, and I decided to hold still for the time being. Or maybe being more petrified than ever decided that for me.

"What's happening?" I asked, pretending to be stuck fast.

"You haven't worked it out?" Seerblight was having a serious gloat. "When Mr Butt visited that handy electrical store on the other side of town, he didn't just take the circuits that your mother needed for my Great Work . . . we replaced the circuits we knew YOU would need to complete your armour with ones created here. Circuits I designed to shut down your clever contraptions, Lady Smyth . . ."

"But how did you know what I needed?" Jem asked.

"Simple." Seerblight turned his cruel gaze onto me. "We hacked into the boy's phone. When you sent him the information by email, we simply opened it and read it."

"So that's why Jem's mail was open on my screen!" I

closed my eyes, so angry with myself. "I didn't suspect a thing!"

"And I installed your sneaky circuits, not noticing anything wrong with them." Jem groaned. "Oh, what a fool!"

"You are too hard on yourself, Lady Smyth." Seerblight's eyes were bright as he came closer. "You have proved most inventive under difficult circumstances. I respect that."

"Watch out, Jem," I said, trying to sound brave. "Sounds like he wants to ask you out on a date!"

"No!" Sir Guy was straining so hard to be free, shaking inside his armour. "Stay away from her, vile fiend!"

"You seek to order me? I, who hold the fate of the entire world in my hands?" With his gauntlet, Seerblight cuffed the helpless Sir Guy about his ghostly chops; with a surge of anger, I wanted to throw myself at him and hit him back – but knew that probably wouldn't help the situation. "I'll tell you what . . . How would you like to know about my secret project on the floor above? How would you like to find out just what it is?" Seerblight had produced some kind of small, sleek remote control from his robes. "My wisdom and genius will change the face of the world forever."

"Wisdom and genius?!" Jem shouted. "You have only ever stolen knowledge from others all your long life!"

"It's a strategy that has worked well for me. And now, at last, my goal is within my grasp. Ultimate power." He pressed a red button on his remote control. "Power over all, as none before me have dreamed possible . . ."

A rumbling noise started up from the floor above us, rising over the iron squeal and grunt of giant cogwheels as they turned. The ceiling began to crack and flake overhead – then seemed to dissolve completely as Seerblight raised both flickering arms above him.

I stared in terrified awe as, in a blaze of unearthly light that made the best CGI effects seem like something knocked up on an old smartphone, a ma-hoosive telescope thing was revealed on the floor above. Protruding impossibly from the wall above us, it seemed sculpted from night-black stone and looked for all the world like a giant bazooka. A telescopic sight sat on the top of it – a long red tube with sparkling glass at either end, plugged into the stone body with a thick black cable. I realised what that part reminded me of – it was a larger version of the scanner from Mum's **BRIAN™** device. Sinister symbols glowed and flickered in the stonework along one side.

"What the goodness me flippington is that?" I whispered (though, since my mum was unconscious at the time, I might have said something ruder).

"This . . . is the most marvellous weapon ever devised!" Seerblight was trembling with glee. "It is my salt-of-igneous CANNON – almost fully charged, it is trained upon the nearest large city. As Jupiter and Venus come into conjunction, as my earthly form reaches its 1000th birthday, so the city shall be bombarded with essence of what you would call 'pow-powder' – and vanish from human senses forever!"

I stared at him. "A whole *city* turned invisible?"

"Yes!" Seerblight gave a skeletal grin. "And that will be but the start of my attack."

"So you will reverse your own invisibility, heal yourself, be fully solid once more and then hold the world to ransom," Jem reasoned. "If the powers that be won't give you what you want, you will make them into phantoms, like us. Am I close?"

"Oh, come now, Lady Smyth! I thought you were cleverer than the rest?" His eyes burned at her through his scrying specs. "I do not wish to be 'healed'! Why should I choose to run my body on food and water? To battle the infirmities of old age as I have to now – elixir or not? To risk accidental harm upon my person at any time? Pah! Why would I choose such an inefficient state of being?" He shook his head. "Oh, no. I knew from the moment I took my elixir that one day I would turn 'invisible', as you call it. And I knew I must be prepared for that day."

Jem frowned. "To endure as an insubstantial phantom forever more, while the world progresses without you?"

"Only a madman would choose such a thing," said Sir Guy.

"Have you not worked it out yet?" Seerblight stared round at us. "I have no interest in blackmailing humans by turning them invisible."

"But . . ." Sir Guy stared. "We thought you wanted to rule the world."

"Oh, I do. I *do* want to rule the world." Seerblight nodded. "But I do NOT want to rule the people who inhabit it."

"Uh-oh," I murmured.

"I have scanned everything in the area of that city for the pow-powder ray to make invisible – everything EXCEPT human beings." He smiled. "Imagine it – buildings and forests and animals. Lakes and rivers and mountains. All of them, transformed and taken away. For, with an unlimited amount of pow-powder, I can transform all things!"

Sir Guy stared. "You mean . . . you want to make *everything* invisible?"

"That is correct. *EVERYTHING!* I shall snatch reality away from the physical plane of perception." Seerblight sneered, as if he found even looking at such idiots as us distasteful. "But I shall NOT transform the humans who crowd this world, who pollute it and devour it and destroy it daily. Oh, no. *They* will find themselves left behind, dwelling in a world of nothing."

"But you've spent so long searching for the cure to pow-powder's effects, trying to reverse it," Jem argued. "Why?"

"Inevitably, when scanning and zapping such large areas, mistakes will creep in. Certain unwanted organisms will be turned invisible, too – a child here, a family there . . ." Seerblight shrugged. "With the cure in my control, I will simply expel them back to their own world where everything they need for survival is out of reach!" He gave a gruesome cackle. "No food! No water! The entire population of the old world will swiftly thirst and starve and die while I, and my world, will endure FOREVER!"

CHAPTER TWENTY-FIVE

World's End

"Ye gods, man," cried Jem, "but this is more monstrous than any plot ever conceived! You wish to freeze the world in a single, unending moment of time?"

"And then rebuild it as I see fit." Seerblight nodded, his head flickering between solid and see-through. "Correct."

I could hardly take it all in. We'd assumed Seerblight was like us, wanting to make himself physical again. Instead, the nutter wanted just the reverse, and was all set to inflict invisibility on the entire world.

"But this planet is massive," I argued, still not moving, pretending my rubbish armour was jammed. "You can't transform all of it at once."

"Of course not. Only a city or two at a time." He sighed. "My cannons must be transported to every corner of the globe to do their work."

"But they'll be attacked by human soldiers!" said Sir Guy. "They'll be destroyed!"

"Not with armoured warriors such as YOU to protect them. Warriors I shall first observe in battle, just as I have observed you. Warriors I shall hand-pick from the greatest armies and turn into armoured ghosts . . ." Seerblight laughed softly as he turned to Jem. "And YOU will be in charge. You have done a fine job with limited resources. Once I grant you *endless* resources, you will do so much better . . ."

"No!" Jem shouted. "I will not serve you!"

"You shall! You EACH shall serve me – for if you don't, the others shall be tortured for ever more!" Seerblight wheezed. "I shall need slaves, you see, to care for me in this new world." He gestured at Mum. "And scientists like her will be most important, too, as I refashion my new domain:

the planet once known as Earth . . . soon to be known as SEERBLIGHT'S STAR!"

"He's a total looper," I wailed. And yet his horrific plans were on the verge of coming true. How could we hope to stop him? My only chance was to take him by surprise. I could still move. I could still fight. I could do this!

Could I?

"You call me mad when the lives of everyone and everything in creation are in my hands, to preserve or destroy?" Gazing up at his giant pow-powder cannon, Seerblight walked a little closer towards me and laughed. "I am no looper, as you so childishly put it. I . . . am . . . a GOD!"

With a muttered prayer to someone else entirely, I threw myself forward, hoping to catch Seerblight off guard. It worked! For a moment, I actually saw surprise on his face.

Then I planted a fist full of WC there!

Seerblight fell over backwards. Desperate to seize the advantage, I grabbed hold of his arm and tried to bend it behind his back. I would force him to destroy this cannon, to let Mum go, to set free my friends. I would . . .

Arrgh! How the heck would I do any of this?

"Mum?" I turned to her.

She wasn't there.

HUH?

I guess I lost concentration for a moment. Seerblight pulled free of my grip, spun round and yanked off my helmet. WHOOSH. His gauntleted hand swung towards my unprotected face. I barely ducked in time. He snarled and grabbed me by the neck, the metal of the gauntlet closing round my throat. I gasped with pain, dangling in the air.

Then I saw, over his shoulder, where my mum had got to. She was up on her feet and working like a demon – a demon with a screwdriver, to be precise – on Sir Guy's armour! And I guess she'd been fiddling with those faulty circuits and got them working because suddenly—

"I AM FREE AGAIN!" Sir Guy came bounding forward, his Lance-a-Lot at the ready. It did not work as a fiery tool, but it still made a fairly awesome bat as he brought it down on top of Seerblight's evil head.

"*Gahhhh!*" Seerblight was sent staggering backwards, and dropped me to the floor. "You fools think you can stop me? You cannot!" Angrily, he pulled out his remote control. "There is still an hour until my 1000th birthday dawns, but you know what? I've *never* been able to wait for my presents!" With a mad laugh, he hit a button on the remote and the huge, stone pow-powder cannon began to pulse with a raging red light above us. A noise like an alien gargling started up, and a ghostly mist began to gather at the business end of Seerblight's great and terrible weapon, still pointed up at the sky like a colossal telescope.

Staring up from the floor, I felt absolute terror creep through me. "What have you done?"

"The cannon is counting down to activation," Seerblight hissed. "In three minutes, the first great city shall disappear from the Earth! Not just its houses, its shops, its hospitals and skyscrapers, but its cars, its buses, its airports, its reservoirs and water pipes . . ."

"Switch it off!" Sir Guy pointed the lance at him. "Now!"

"No." Seerblight dropped the remote and stamped on it. **PHUT!** It sparked and smoked, squashed flat. "Ha! Now nobody can stop it!"

"NOOOOO!" Sir Guy started forward, but Seerblight pointed at him and – ***ZAPPP!*** – weird white energy sparked from the gauntlet. The knight fell back, reeling.

I tried to spin round and kick Seerblight's legs from under him. But his reactions were too fast – he moved away in a blur and zapped me, too. It felt like fire scooshing along my invisible veins, an intricate pattern of pain flowing through my whole body.

"Noah!" Mum shouted. I saw she'd taken her screwdriver to Jem now, working to free her. But, as she was distracted looking over at me, Seerblight fired his finger again.

"Mum, look out!" The pain was passing – but with my helmet gone there was no metal to amplify my voice. The flare of light sparked off Jem's armour. Its power threw Mum aside . . .

But it also seemed to finish the job she'd started! Jem jerked back into life, in control again. "Evil madman!" she snarled. "I'll see that you do not enjoy your victory!" Her left hand flew to a concealed button at her hip and launched a conical flask of steaming orange brightness at Seerblight.

"Ha!" The old wizard caught it with his gauntleted hand. "You think some thin chemical concoction can harm me?" He broke it – then gasped as his metal glove was engulfed in red-hot goo. "*What?*"

"It's not chemicals," Jem shouted. "It's lava, taken from your own trap downstairs!"

"*Gahhh!*" While Seerblight tried to wipe the molten mess from his sizzling hand, Sir Guy struck him aside with a swing of the lance that smashed into the old man's shoulder. Seerblight gasped and fell to the floor.

"Well done, Sir Guy! You, too, Jem." Wearily, I pushed myself up onto my elbows. "You . . . did great."

"As did you, lad. But we were too slow." Sir Guy hung his head. "Too late to stop that foul churl!"

Above us, the gargling noise from the cannon began to build. The lights pulsed faster and the smoke at the tip began to thicken. I crawled over to check on my mum. There was just enough metallic dust on my hands for me to be able to hold her. "Hey, Mum," I whispered. She was still breathing, and seemed fast asleep.

I felt numb. In what – maybe two minutes now? – the world would be rocked by the disappearance of an entire city. Millions of people would be left homeless. Thousands would fall from the upper storeys of disappearing buildings . . . Thousands more would die in hospitals as their beds vanished beneath them . . . Thousands more would—

Enough! We get the picture, yes?

"We can't give up!" Jem cried. "We MUST stop that cannon from firing!"

"We are the only ones that can," Sir Guy agreed.

"NO ONE CAN!" Sprightly for a thousand-year-old, Seerblight rolled over – and pulled a sonic blaster from the folds of his cloak.

With the volume turned up to the max, he opened fire.

The noise tore through me, set every atom quivering, set every nerve on fire. I saw Jem jumping and twitching and flattening out as if kicked about by a herd of taser-wielding elephants. Sir Guy was thrown high up into the air – he smashed his armoured head on Seerblight's cannon, did a double somersault upwards and landed on top of it like a metal sock slung over a very thick washing line.

When the sound stopped, my body felt broken by the violence of the vibrations and my invisible head was ringing like mad. I could barely move, barely think. But I saw that Seerblight was back on his feet, the half-melted gauntlet now smoking on the floor, a leering smile back on his face.

"No!" I called feebly. "No!"

Jem and Sir Guy were stirring just as weakly. Mum was flat on her face. Maloney neighed desperately, his rigid armour rocking as he tried, and failed, to move.

"All your efforts have come to nothing." Seerblight was exultant. "The end of this world begins in a handful of heartbeats. Sixty seconds to go! Fifty-nine . . . fifty-eight . . . fifty-seven . . ."

CHAPTER TWENTY-SIX

The End

As the light show built above me . . .

As the cannon pulsed with horrible energy . . .

As its eerie vibrations shook through Seerblight's tower . . .

As the smoke was sucked up inside the huge, glowing nozzle and the final seconds ticked away . . .

I rolled over, unable to watch.

And found myself face to face with the scanning bit of Mum's **BRIAN™ Zap-and-Scanner**, knocked from my grip just after I'd scanned Seerblight . . .

Just after I'd scanned Seerblight!

"Fifty-two!" Lost in the wonders of his victory, Seerblight went on chanting his creepy countdown. "Fifty-one . . ."

"Jem!" I crawled painfully towards her. "Check out that cannon thing!"

She looked across in a daze. "Funnily enough, Noah, I

have already noticed it."

"I mean, study it. Look at its connections and stuff. Mum helped him build it, right? It's based on her technology." I reached Jem's side. "And here's Mum's scanner-gadget. It plugs into her smaller-sized pow-powder zapper, lets her choose what gets invisibled!"

Jem nodded. "Most ingenious, I am sure."

"You don't get me!" I hissed. "He's used a bigger scanner to scan the city and plugged it into the cannon so the city gets zapped with pow-powder. But what if we could SWITCH the scanners . . ."

"Of course!" Jem breathed. "Then Seerblight himself would become the cannon's target!" She peered up through the smoke and light at the cannon's underside.

"Forty!" Seerblight gave a mad cackle and crossed to the large window, ready to watch the show. "Thirty-eight . . . thirty-seven . . ."

"As your mother built both machines, and they work on the same principle, they *should* be compatible . . ." Jem stared at me helplessly. "But there's no time to get up there and see for sure!"

"NEIGH!" Maloney said loudly. **"NEIGHHH!"**

"What . . . what is it, boy?" called Sir Guy weakly from above us. "Daddy's trying to sleep . . ."

And it hit me like a metal fist – Sir Guy was lying on top of the cannon!

I gave Maloney a frantic thumbs up, and called: "Hey, Sir Guy! It's Noah. Now you're awake, you have to do something for us."

"Thirty-one . . . thirty." Seerblight turned round crossly. "There is nothing you can do!" he snapped. 'You are powerless, you hear me? Helpless!"

"NEIGHHHHHH!" With one last, superheroic effort, Maloney managed to move in his malfunctioning armour. And wow, HOW he moved, tipping forward onto his front legs like a gymnast doing a handstand! Sparks flew from his full metal Bad Saddle as it ejected, leaping from his back, flying through the air . . .

And smashing into Seerblight's back, crushing him against the thick glass window like a swatted fly. "Erk!" the sorcerer moaned.

"YEIGH!" said Maloney, tipping back down onto all four legs again.

"You're a star, boy!" I told him.

But now, with less than half a minute left, it was down to the three of us.

"Sir Guy!" Jem called. "If you reach down to your left, you will find a thick black cable joining the telescopic sight on top of the cannon to the cannon itself."

"The what?" Sir Guy boomed.

"The red metal thing with the glassy bit on the end!"

I yelled back.

"Ah . . . yes! Got it!" Sir Guy called. "Shall I mangle it?"

"NO!" Jem cringed. "Unplug it from the telescopic sight! Be careful!"

"Careful?" Sir Guy sounded puzzled. "What is this strange word, 'careful' . . . ?"

"Never mind!" I got up, weighed the little scanner in my hands. "Unplug the cable *without* mangling it – and plug it into the thing I'm going to throw up to you."

"You are going to throw up at me, lad? Can you not use a bucket—?"

"I'm going to throw a gadget up to you!"

I screamed. How long did we have now – twenty seconds? Fifteen? "Are you ready?"

"*Mais oui!*"

Jem took one end of the scanner; I took the other. We looked at each other . . . counted quickly to three . . . and hurled it upwards into the smoke.

"Got it!" Sir Guy shouted. "Thank you. 'Tis very nice."

"PLUG THE CABLE INTO IT!" we shrieked.

"Very well. Now where is the hole . . ."

"Quickly!" I squeaked.

"Let me have a look . . ."

"Just do it!" Jem begged him.

"Is this it? No . . ."

Maloney whinnied in despair.

"Whatever you were planning, you are too late!" Seerblight had got back to his feet, his face bruised, his eyes shining with malevolence. "Three! Two! One! ZEROOOOOOOOOOOOO!"

There was nothing more we could do but watch. The pow-powder cannon seemed to swell as if drawing in some enormous demonic breath, and then, finally, horribly, terrifyingly:

It fired.

The light show was a blinder, almost literally. A chaos of colour and breathtaking brightness.

Noooooooooo

Seerblight went up like a Guy Fawkes dummy on a nuclear bonfire!

And when the light finally faded, and the vibrations died away, and the cannon fell silent and still . . . there was no trace of him left at all.

Jem smiled slowly. "It . . . actually . . . worked!"

"What did I do?" called Sir Guy.

"You swapped Seerblight's scan-target for Mum's!" I told him. "So, instead of the cannon firing its pow-powder at the city, it fired it at Seerblight!"

Jem nodded. "He took enough pow-powder to turn a whole city invisible . . . enough to vanish him a million times over!"

"He's gone." Mum was awake now, sitting up. "Seerblight is gone forever."

"YEIGHHH!" Maloney cheered.

But my smile faltered as I looked at Mum and realised she couldn't see me. "Only thing is . . . we're still gone, too."

But Mum could see my armour, at least. She crouched beside the pile of random metal and gave it a gentle hug. "Don't worry, Noah. Seerblight forced me to come up with the way to reverse pow-powder, remember? The formula is in the chilled cabinet, ready to rock. I'll get you right back to normal." She looked around. "I'll get all of you back to normal. Then we'll destroy that cannon and all the rest of the pow-powder so it can never be used again."

Mum smiled in the direction of my face, and I smiled back with actual, proper happiness for the first time since I'd become invisible. Then she turned to Lady J beside me. "I heard Noah call you Jem . . . so I'm thinking you're Lady Jemima Smyth?"

Jem curtseyed politely.

"I . . . thought you might like this back." Mum pulled Jem's old diary from the pocket of her stained lab coat. "Letting me read it caused one or two, er, issues . . ."

"But, in the end, it happened to save the world." Jem took it, turned to me and smiled. "Good can come from even the biggest disasters, you see?"

"I see." Then I shuddered. "But I'd rather not see *that* thing ever again!"

Jem crossed to the lava still bubbling on Seerblight's gauntlet and dropped the diary into it. It burst into flames, the secrets on its pages lost forever.

With a nod of satisfaction, Mum picked up her screwdriver and went over to Maloney, started working to set him free.

"Cured," said Jem quietly, looking very moved. "Oh, Noah, we shall be cured! After so, so long, I will be able to change my clothes . . . drink tea . . ."

"DRINK ALE!" cried Sir Guy.

"And we shall begin to age again." Jem shook her head in wonderment. "The passing of the years will leave their mark."

I nodded. "I guess if you weren't cured, you'd live forever?"

"No, Noah. One might endure forever, as Seerblight hoped, but one would not *live*." She nodded sagely. "True living is all that we put into the years – and all we take in return."

"Pish! Your worthy wisdom is throwing the party vibe, milady!" Sir Guy dropped down from the cannon and whumped her affectionately on the shoulder. "Let us get ready to wassail and fill the mead cup with ale, brandy, cider and wine. And then more ale! The world is saved!"

As Maloney was freed by Mum, he stamped a metal hoofbeat out on the floor. Sir Guy started beatboxing, then burst into a booming rap:

"Victory is ours!
We got the powers!
Invisible Inc. made a mess
of Seerblight Towers!
Scattering ninjas
and blowing up Butt
Saving the world,
now you're seeing us strut!"

To my amazement, Jem suddenly joined in, while Sir Guy got back to his bonkers beatboxing.

"Except you really can't see us
cos of course we're invisible.
Well, soon we'll be solid –
but still indivisible!
Yeah, Momma. Check me out!"

Jem launched into a wild cancan in full spiky armour. It was one of the strangest things I've ever seen.

But as I stared out over the twinkling lights of the stars above and the town below – a town that wouldn't be going anywhere soon – I found myself joining in with the crazy shape-throwing.

Well. They say you should dance like no one's watching, don't they?

And, when you're invisible – or Invisible Incorporated – there's really no excuse not to take that to the max.

EPILOGUE

What Did They Do Next?

LADY JEMIMA SMYTH

Once retired from Invisible Inc., moved into Seerblight's HQ. She employed the beaten, battered ninjas to clear out all the traps, magic and roasted chicken-monsters and had the place converted into the 'Lady Smyth Very Nice School for Scientists', to be run by Professor Trudi Deer (with special half-term 'battle' lessons supplied by Sir Guy deYupp and his pony, Maloney). She then took several science degrees at top universities around the world and became joint head of a secret science research team alongside Professor Hannah-Anna Hongananna and Dr Eric Gooseheart (and, so rumour has it, an alien very fond of hugs known as Little G – see *ALIENS STINK* from Magic Ink Productions).

SIR GUY deYUPP

Once retired from Invisible Inc., founded the world's most successful and spectacular historical re-enactment society with particular attention paid to BATTLES. His debut album, Mansion-master Guy (Feat. Rude Horse and Bad Lady J) Sings Your Favourite Battlefield Ballads reached number one in the 'Battlefield Ballad' chart.

MALONEY the PONY

Once retired from Invisible Inc., became a racehorse and won the Grand National and Triple Crown several years running before retiring from the sport and becoming manager of Sir Guy de Yupp's Splendid Historical Re-enactment Society and occasional guest speaker at the Lady Smyth Very Nice School for Scientists. His book of verse, *Green is the Sugar Lump of Youth*, quickly became a *New York Times* Bestseller.

TRUDI DEER

Never served baked beans to her son again; most times, they cook and eat their meals together. Currently teaching young scientists at the Lady Smyth Very Nice School for Scientists. Also working on her own amazing projects, but remembers to take time off once in a while.

AND WHAT HAPPENED TO THAT BOY . . .?

Noah Deer is out there getting noticed as a writer. He's already written the true story of his experiences with pow-powder – with a little help from co-authors Sir Guy deYupp, Jemima Smyth and Maloney the Pony – and he's sure that many more adventures lie ahead. He plans to write all about those, too . . .

In *visible* ink.

MAGIC INK
READ THIS ONE!
STEVE COLE
A COMIC-STRIP TRIP LIKE NO OTHER!

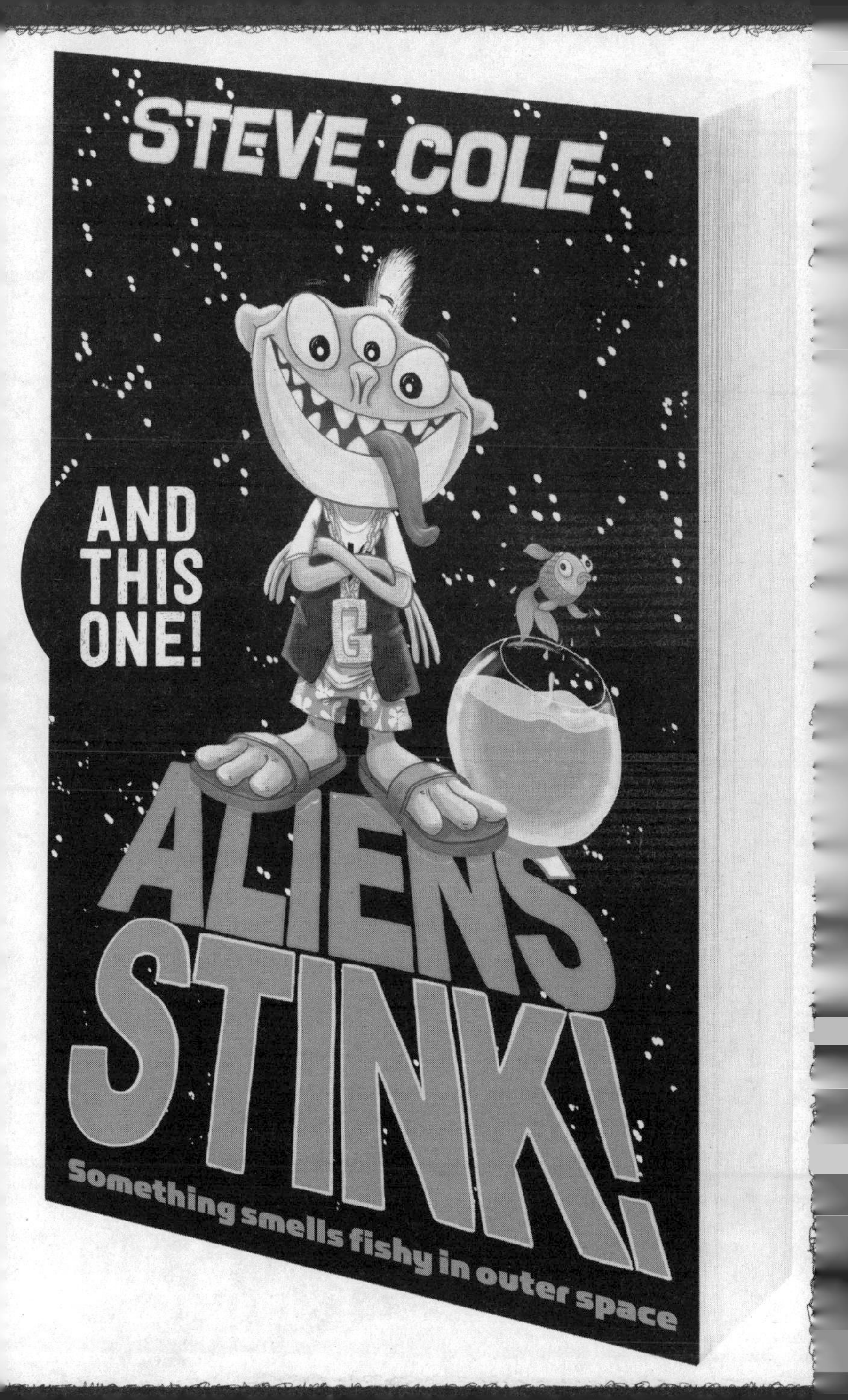
STEVE COLE
AND THIS ONE!
ALIENS STINK!
Something smells fishy in outer space

A BOY. A QUEST.
AND A WHOLE LOT OF MONSTERS!
STOP THOSE MONSTERS!
AND THIS ONE!
STEVE COLE
Author of MAGIC INK 'A cracking read' Sun